THE APPLE EATERS

THE
APPLE EATERS

Ernest Langford

HARBOUR PUBLISHING

HARBOUR PUBLISHING
Box 219
Madeira Park, BC V0N 2H0

Published with the assistance of the Canada Council and the
Government of British Columbia, Cultural Services Branch
Printed and bound in Canada

Canadian Cataloguing in Publication Data

Langford, Ernest, 1920–

The apple eaters

ISBN 1-55017-100-3
I. Title.
PS8573.A555A73 1994   C813'.54   C94-910158-3
PR9199.3.L26A73 1994

To Caroline

Whenever Jimmy Sung, an inveterate classifier of present and past actions, recalls the events of that April day just five years past, he begins by placing himself at the window of the office he occupied above his mother's produce store on East Pender Street in Vancouver.

That afternoon Jimmy had been standing at his post for over an hour, once again asking himself how it had come to pass that a man like himself, who had been a whiz kid all his life and possessed an LL.B. degree (with honours) from a first-class university, could have ended up at age twenty-seven in a crummy office with a secondhand desk, two chairs, a thrift-store manual typewriter, a telephone circa 1960 and a scratched filing cabinet, when his original intention had been to lord it over lesser mortals in a high-tech, oak-panelled office on Howe Street, doling out legal advice to British Columbia's corporate elite at exorbitant fees. But the familiar question was merely rhetorical. The reason Jimmy conducted his dreary legal practice in that shabby little room was because, halfway through his year clerking for a BC Supreme Court judge, he had suddenly run out of steam and ceased being a whiz kid. Consequently, for a few years now, he had been drudging away in his little office, probating wills, conveyancing houses and, more recently, as a result of inserting a one-line notice in the Investigators section of the Yellow Pages and adding the word *Legal*

Researches to the brass plate at the foot of the stairs leading to his office, spying on errant husbands and wives on behalf of spouses convinced their marital partners were bestowing more than innocent glances on young acquaintances of the same or opposite sex.

So what Jimmy was feeling as he stared out the office window on that particular April afternoon was not so much boredom—though heaven knew he was seriously bored—but anxiety, because this state of affairs, rather than being temporary, might just bear a strong resemblance to his future. How could he possibly bring himself to climb the twenty stairs to this office, day in, day out?

Jimmy's gloom had been aggravated that afternoon by his mother Annette reminding him at lunch that all he needed to set himself rocketing to the peak of professional wealth and glory was a healthy, ambitious wife. To set this process in motion, Annette had taken to scanning all post-pubescent young women, including Caucasians, who entered her store. If they passed her initial scrutiny, she blatantly questioned them about their ancestry and financial prospects, stopping just short of pinching cheeks, poking chests, and raising skirts (just to make sure). In her scheme to get Jimmy back on the highway to legal distinction, Annette was enthusiastically assisted by her daughters Julie and Lucille; although Jimmy revered his mother and adored his younger sisters, he nevertheless often wished he had sufficient determination to break away and find his own road.

◆   ◆   ◆

So it is a thoroughly discontented Jimmy Sung who is looking out the office window at the people swarming along East Pender Street when he hears the door creak and open. A woman is silhouetted in the doorway. The way the light is entering the room keeps her face in the shadows, but she appears to be wearing a loose skirt and jacket, the type of clothes Jimmy associates with thrift shops. Inwardly Jimmy groans—this prospective client may be unable to pay for his services.

"Yes? What is it?" he barks, his voice unnecessarily sharp.

"Is this the right place?" the woman tentatively asks.

Now, when Jimmy recalls the scene, he visualizes himself strutting from the window to his desk, resting one hand on it and the other on his hip, before replying, "How can I know whether it is, if I don't know where you wanted to go?" Jimmy does not like to believe he could have behaved in such a pompous and asinine manner. But probably he did. Five years later he still grimaces at the memory.

"James Sung Investigations."

"You have come to the right place. I am James Sung. Please sit." Jimmy stands beside the desk, waiting while the woman crosses from the doorway to arrange herself on the smaller of the two chairs. As she advances, Jimmy reduces his potential client's age from mid-thirties to late teens and changes his mind about her clothes when he recognizes that the outfit she wears is the uniform of an exclusive girls' school and consists of a pleated tartan skirt, white blouse, knee-high socks and a navy blue blazer with the school crest embroidered on the breast pocket.

After seating himself, Jimmy stares back at the first person of Caucasian origin to have entered his office since he opened it four years ago. She is perched on the edge of her chair, hands folded in her lap trying to look prim, a very difficult assignment given her long perfect legs and a skirt that does not get any closer than three inches from the tops of her knees. But neither her legs, large blue-grey eyes, high chiselled cheekbones, full red lips, nor heart-shaped face is her most striking feature, at least the way Jimmy looks at her. No, it is the hair; the most unusual long, bronze-coloured hair.

"Thank goodness the rain's stopped," she says, and Jimmy agrees that seventy-two hours of steady rain is a bit much, but it is Vancouver, after all. He then waits patiently for her to explain herself. Instead, she remarks that this is her first visit to Chinatown.

Jimmy bows his head in acknowledgement of the important occasion.

"You've come to consult me about a problem?" Jimmy often finds that the people who enter his office assume he already knows their reason for being there.

The girl ignores Jimmy's question and says she had difficulty locating his office. "Fortunately the lady in the store downstairs helped me."

"That's not surprising. She's my mother."

The girl looks at Jimmy as if she finds it hard to believe he could actually have a mother. Then she smiles and enthusiastically says, "She's very nice." Jimmy agrees, while noting the teeth revealed by the girl's smile look as if they have been cared for by a solicitous dentist from the first moment they popped out of her gums and began chewing the finest available foods.

"So, what can I do for you?"

"It's about—" she begins.

"Yes," Jimmy nudges, "yes?"

"That police officer was wrong. He thinks my brother—" She halts again while Jimmy, snatching at the hint, flips recent media reports through his mind until he finds one concerning the dead body of a UBC student discovered on the rocks beneath Lions Gate Bridge. (Having so much free time allows Jimmy to scan every square centimetre of copy in the Vancouver newspapers. Desperation occasionally drives him even to note each and every item listed in public auction notices and to study details of landscaping projects open to tender. He is the kind of guy who remembers the closing dates).

"Martin would never do anything like that," she firmly states. "Never." As if to emphasize her point, she angles her head and squints at Jimmy. "He wasn't that kind of person."

He nods solemnly, and politely asks for her name. "It's Janet Elizabeth MacDougail. Pronounced Mac-Dou-*gail*. I always have to explain how to pronounce my surname," she adds irritably. "My brother's name is—I mean, was—Martin John MacDougail."

She suddenly appears suspicious of what he is writing on his yellow legal pad.

Jimmy smiles, holds up the pad, and explains he is recording the date and time of day, her name and the name of her brother.

She crosses her legs with exaggerated slowness. "You won't write down anything personal about me, will you?"

"Yes!" Jimmy blurts, suddenly finding something of immense interest on the wall to his right. To himself he thinks, the last person I saw who lifted her knee that high was a drum majorette. "I mean, no!"

"Well then," she says with a little pout, "I guess it's all right."

Having composed himself, Jimmy ventures a glance at her over the rims of his spectacles. Jimmy has 20-20 vision and has plain lenses in the glasses, which he wears only when doing business, because he believes prospective clients associate wearing spectacles with professional diligence and expertise.

"Martin would never do anything like that," she repeats.

"Quite so," Jimmy mutters. "Do you live in Vancouver?"

"Of course." She supplies him with the address of a house in the heart of Shaughnessy, Vancouver's most exclusive west-side neighbourhood. "I live with my grandmother. Our parents died when Martin and I were little."

"I see," Jimmy says, even though he has as yet to hear anything that might explain why the girl is sitting in his office. He nods and smiles, then politely says, "May I ask how old you are?"

He continues to smile at her as she speculatively eyes him before saying defiantly, "I'm seventeen, going on eighteen." Jimmy records the numerals on his pad, imagining a spectral, grim-faced elderly woman shimmering behind the girl's chair and forming the words "I never pay for unauthorized services", while the girl emphatically adds, "And I know exactly what I'm doing."

"No doubt," Jimmy agrees, then cautiously asks if her grandmother knows she has come to see him. The girl shakes her head and Jimmy notices that her hair ripples as water does when unseen, mysterious creatures move below its surface.

"Gran's not knowing doesn't matter though. I know why I am here."

"Of course, however—"

"It's because that police officer was wrong, " she angrily interrupts. "That's why I looked in the Yellow Pages and found your name."

"That's very gratifying," Jimmy says, although he has trouble understanding why a person named MacDougail would select an investigator named Sung. She guesses what Jimmy is thinking and she proffers an explanation that seems totally nonsensical to Jimmy, but apparently makes perfect sense to her. "Gran gave me an Alfred Sung jacket last Christmas and I thought you might be related to him."

"I'm afraid not," Jimmy murmurs. "I'm sorry."

"That's all right," she magnanimously tells him. "Gran says we must always make the best of things. Does your mother say things like that?"

"Frequently," Jimmy says. "Mother's favourite expression is 'It's no big deal'."

"Well, I suppose most things aren't really big deals, are they?" she airily comments, while Jimmy tries to come up with a way to direct the conversation into a more productive channel.

"The Vancouver police have a good reputation," he says.

"I've absolutely no idea what they have," she acidly remarks. "I just know the officer who came to our house didn't speak to anyone except Granny."

"And you think he should have spoken with you?"

"Yes."

"Why?" When she does not answer, Jimmy says. "Could you have given him some information he couldn't have gotten from your grandmother?"

She looks intently at Jimmy for a few moments. "I don't know. But at least he could have asked me. Couldn't he?"

"Yes. Although you could have said you wanted to speak with him."

Jimmy's harmless remark produces what seems to him an unreasoned burst of anger. "Do you expect me to run after people who don't want to talk to me?"

"No, but on the other hand the police can only act on information given them,".

"I don't care what they do. I don't want anything to do with them."

"Of course. Do you happen to know what the police officer told your grandmother?"

"He said . . ." She stops and Jimmy can see the muscles in her throat convulse. It's a lovely throat. "He said . . . Martin had . . . that Martin had . . . committed suicide. But it's not true. I know it's not true. Martin would never do anything like that."

"I see," Jimmy says, wondering if he sees anything at all.

"That's why I'm going to employ you," she says.

At this point in the exchange Jimmy decides to place a few hard facts before Ms. Janet MacDougail. "You understand that investigations are costly," he begins.

"I know that!" she snaps. "I'm not stupid."

"I'm sure you're not, but we have to consider who will pay for the work."

"How much do you charge?" she asks flatly.

"Well . . ." Jimmy equivocates, "it depends on the extent of the investigation."

"You don't have to worry about being paid. I'll have no trouble getting money from Gran."

Jimmy now feels this young woman must be brought down to earth. He leans across the desk and points a finger at her, like a judge gearing up to deliver a reproving lecture to a habitual criminal. "Let's stop right here, Ms. MacDougail. Suppose your grandmother does agree to a private investigation into your brother's death. That is the reason, I assume, that you've come to see me. Isn't it?" She nods agreement. "How can you be so certain your grandmother will advance the money?"

"I know she will, Mr. Sung."

"Please call me Jimmy."

"All right. And you can call me Janet."

"Okay, suppose your grandmother agrees to pay. Wouldn't she prefer someone of Caucasian origin to conduct the investigation?"

"Oh no!" she indignantly protests. "Gran isn't like that at all. She's not one of *those* people!" Jimmy supposes she is referring to the minority of Canadians who voice the racism that the majority silently support. "Besides, it's my money. And Martin's."

"So you're quite sure your grandmother will cover the costs? Even if the investigation adds up to, say, thousands of dollars?"

She stares at Jimmy for a moment, then slumps to one side of the chair and commences to chew her lower lip and rub her nose, all the while looking like a girl. Then she turns into a woman as she crosses her legs again. Jimmy is surprised this time to realize he missed the flash of pale blue panties the last time. "Do you have a cut rate?" she finally asks, as Jimmy studiously examines the black-framed evidence of his academic and legal qualifications decorating the wall to the left.

Turning back, he is relieved to see she is once again sitting straight in the chair. "No, I don't," replies Jimmy, "and you must realize that suicide is—"

"I've already told you. Martin did not—" She suddenly stops and looks around the room as if seeking suitable words to describe her brother's death. She continues. "Anyway . . . I know Gran will give me the money."

"Don't you think you should discuss this matter with your grandmother first? To be on the safe side?".

"All right." She smiles. "I will." She rises to her feet, extends her right hand, and says, "I just know you'll help me."

"You will discuss this whole matter with your grandmother, won't you?" says Jimmy, moving to the door.

"Of course," she says as she passes him to stand in the hall. "May I use your bathroom, please?" Jimmy points down the hall, then watches as Janet walks along the narrow passage. Her stride is that of the upper-class Caucasian female, assertive and confident, the movement of a person who never questions her right to walk anywhere, whenever and however she chooses.

Back in his office, Jimmy stands at the window and looks out into the street, where the pallid late afternoon sunlight, now emerging from dense clouds, is illuminating the interior of stores across the street. He can see his sister Julie standing at the cash register of her husband's variety store. Jimmy smiles and thinks that Julie is the one person he knows who has fulfilled a childhood dream. Once, as a birthday present, Julie had received a miniature grocery store, complete with shelves, boxes, tin cans and, above all, a working cash register filled with play money. Julie was enthralled with the gift and told her mother when she grew up she wanted to own a real store. This goal she achieved through her marriage to Bill Wong, owner and operator of Wong's Variety and, in Jimmy's opinion, the dullest man in all of Canada. Now Jimmy sees Julie opening and closing the cash register while animatedly chatting with customers. It never ceases to amaze him that any person living in a world that mirrors itself to him as little more than a maelstrom of individual suffering and collective social discontent could be as content as his sister Julie so obviously is.

Jimmy turns from the window as Janet MacDougail reappears in the doorway, and again is struck by how mature she looks from a distance. "What is the easiest way for me to get home?" she asks. "I'll have to walk because I don't know the bus routes."

"You mean you walked here all the way from Shaughnessy?"

"Yes."

Jimmy hesitates a few seconds. "I'll drive you."

"You don't have to do that," she says earnestly. "I'm a fast walker."

Jimmy points to his expensive wrist watch, Annette's gift on the occasion of his graduation from law school. "It's closing time for me anyway. I'll spin you home in Mother's Corolla. It's easier to handle in rush hour than my car." This is plain bullshit. All Jimmy possesses in the way of an automobile is the three-hundred-dollar beater now parked in the alley at the rear of Annette's store. Even to look at the thing acutely embarrasses him. It actually runs, but he can never be sure when it might abruptly stop, usually in the middle of a busy intersection or on a hill that even tots on tricycles scale without much difficulty. Originally, Jimmy had ridden in this car as a passenger, its owner being a student studying for an advanced degree in the Faculty of Education at UBC. Jimmy—still a whiz kid then—found him a bit slow on the uptake, but nevertheless suffered him as intellectually superior people do those who are less brainy than themselves; without fail, he contributed his share of gas and oil to the running of the car. Its owner had inherited the vehicle through a tangled web of relatives, which meant it was pretty far gone by the time he offered it to Jimmy.

Getting the ignition key for the Corolla means he has to introduce Janet to his mother. Annette immediately gives Janet a glossy-skinned Spartan apple and in her not-so-covert way proceeds to inspect her marital potential. Jimmy of course realizes what is going on, but Janet is blissfully unaware she is being inspected and concentrates on eating the apple as rapidly as possible, juice glistening on her chin. While this is going on, Lucille strolls in, sums up the situation, and walks over to slip her arm through Jimmy's. "Hello," she coos at Janet, "I'm Lucille, Jimmy's younger sister."

Often when Jimmy looks at Lucille he thinks he can see Annette as she may have been before bearing children had thickened her body and years of relentless labour had engraved lines on her face; though for Jimmy the similarity ends there, for while Annette is almost obsessively energetic and good-natured, Lucille tends to be lazy and becomes horribly waspish when thwarted—not that these shortcomings prevent Jimmy from adoring Lucille. Although he sees his sister every day of his life, after she has been out of his sight, even for a few hours, he catches his breath when he again glimpses her Hong-Kong-movie-heroine face. Jimmy loves his sister Julie for her virtues, but passionately adores Lucille for her beauty, even though he believes Lucille is not as deserving of his adoration as Julie, for she possesses neither Julie's intelligence nor goodness of heart. His preference for Lucille shames Jimmy, because he believes Julie's goodness should take precedence over Lucille's beauty, but he finds no matter how hard he tries he cannot alter the way he values his sisters. Lucille, who is twenty-two years old and taking art courses at a school on Granville Island, talks of opening a shop where she will design and sell clothes. But Jimmy doubts if this venture will ever materialize since Lucille seems content just drifting from day to day, gossiping with friends and ignoring the attentions of the numerous young men who pursue her.

As Jimmy waits for his mother to give him the keys to her car, he finds himself entertaining the treasonous notion that in Janet his sister Lucille may have met her Caucasian match.

Much to Jimmy's embarrassment, Julie appears from her shop across the street to take his other arm. He introduces her to Janet. "Fortunately these two are the only sisters I have. I wouldn't know what to do with more." Eventually he manages to detach Janet from the family circle, quickly packs her into Annette's white Corolla and drives south along Main Street, all the while acutely aware of Janet's body beside him and of the scent of her soap and cologne. "Why are you so certain your brother did not kill himself?" he asks.

"Because he promised to take me for a ride in his new sports car."

Jimmy considers her reply for a moment in silence, wondering whether she is ingenuous or just an airhead. He tries another tack.

"Did you get along well with your brother?"

"Most of the time. Though sometimes I bugged him."

"Why?"

"I don't know. Maybe me being a girl. Sometimes I think Martin wished he had a brother instead of me."

"Didn't your brother like girls?"

"Oh yes. He was very popular with them."

Jimmy stops at the light on Broadway and is surprised when Janet points to the opposite street corner and informs him she saw her brother there one evening, talking to a girl. The light turns green, and after crossing Broadway Jimmy draws into the curb and stops. "Is there a particular reason your brother shouldn't have been at that location?" he asks.

"I don't know. I asked Martin about it and he said he'd never been anywhere near there."

"I see," Jimmy says, trying to knit together the fragments of information he has received so far.

"I was going home with Gran after a boring symphony concert. Gran always makes me go with her. Beasley—that's our driver—was taking a friend of Gran's home. That's why we happened to be driving along there."

"You realize you could have been mistaken."

"I wasn't!" She flushes angrily. Since Broadway and Main is a prostitutes' stroll, maybe it is not too surprising that Martin MacDougail would want to deny being there. Jimmy senses that Janet is coming to the same conclusion when she asks, "Do you suppose Martin was talking to one of those . . . you know . . . hookers?"

"Well, prostitutes do hang around here. I saw a couple of them while we were waiting for the light to change." Jimmy becomes excessively casual, trying to sound as though he has seen nothing more out-of-the-way than two stray cats loping across the street. He does not want to shock Janet, nor to say anything that might lead her to think he is familiar with the activities of Vancouver whores.

"But Martin would never want anything to do with a girl like that."

Jimmy thinks there may be problems ahead if Janet MacDougail holds too many beliefs concerning her brother's moral impeccability.

"How old was Martin?" he asks as he puts the car into gear and moves out into traffic.

"Twenty-three."

"Did he live at home?"

"Oh, no. He moved into his own apartment after he started at UBC."

"What was he majoring in?"

"Business administration. Granny said it would come in useful when Martin joined the company."

Jimmy turns the car at an intersection and melds into the

flow of traffic going west on 41st Avenue. "So, your brother was going be employed by a family company, is that right?"

"Yes, but I really don't know much about it." This doesn't surprise Jimmy. A girl like Janet could not be expected to know about business matters; she was likely being groomed for marriage to a man from a well-heeled local family of her own class, thus solidifying her family's financial and social status in the community. Jimmy glances sideways at Janet and thinks she is quite well suited for the life he suspects is being planned for her.

"I suppose your brother had plenty of friends," Jimmy says as he halts at a red light on Granville Street.

"Lots."

"Men and women?"

"Mostly girls. Martin said girls liked him because of his sports cars."

"Sensible of them," Jimmy comments, reflecting on the connection between his own car and dearth of female acquaintances. "Did he have a special friend?"

"He may have." She frowns. Jimmy decides there may be a lot about her brother's life that Janet MacDougail doesn't know.

After they cross Granville she directs him to a street on which lofty trees meet to form a sombre arch over the pavement. Janet MacDougail tells Jimmy to stop at the entrance to a driveway where the house is obscured by a tall, thick laurel hedge. Jimmy offers Janet his business card. "You can telephone me after you've talked with your grandmother."

She nods, takes the card, half opens the door, then closes it again. "Mr. Sung, I mean, Jimmy, do you—" She stops, and Jimmy guesses what she is trying to say. "Do you think . . . well . . . do you think . . . Martin might have been doing something wrong the night I saw him with that girl?"

Because Jimmy has no idea how to respond to the question, he procrastinates. "I should remind you of something, Janet. Your brother said you were mistaken about seeing him there."

"I didn't make a mistake!" She now watches Jimmy closely, waiting to hear what he is going to say next.

"Look, right now I'm in no position to give you an opinion about your brother."

"I know that."

Jimmy realizes he must be careful. "You mustn't ask me to make value judgments. That's not my job. If I'm going to work for you, it will be to gather information, not to evaluate people's behaviour."

"Suppose one of your sisters saw you talking to a girl like that?"

Jimmy decides he has had enough of Janet MacDougail for one day. He is beginning to think she is one of those infuriating people (like Lucille) who are always attempting to reduce abstract social and moral questions to a personal level, invariably demanding absolute judgments from professional people (like himself) who make their living dealing in equivocations. "That isn't the issue here, so you shouldn't drag it in. And there's another point: you may not approve of what those young women do, but it's not illegal. After all, they're just trying to make a living."

Janet gets out of the car and glares at him. "I don't care what they do." She spits out the words. "I just care about what my brother did."

Jimmy nods and smiles appeasement. "Yes, yes, I appreciate that. So why not discuss it with your grandmother and then telephone me tomorrow."

"I'm not sure I want to employ you any more." She turns and runs up the driveway, disappearing from Jimmy's sight. He sighs, pockets his spectacles and returns to Union Street, where he is assailed with questions from Annette and Lucille. By now Jimmy has a throbbing headache and is thoroughly depressed. He tells them to forget Janet MacDougail. Nothing is going to come of her visit anyway.

2

Jimmy Sung has a bugbear hypothesis. Bugbears, he claims, explain why horses don't win races for punters on particular days, why average folks don't end up millionaires and why rain falls on picnics. Most people, Jimmy theorizes, want to be able to glide through life, experiencing maximum pleasure with a minimum investment of effort; when that simple formula rarely works out in their everyday lives, people invent bugbears to explain why. Bugbears, the way he figures it, are escape hatches enabling people to flee just minutes before their fragile vessels of hope and belief are engulfed by waves of futility and despair. But bugbears must not be confused with scapegoats; a bugbear offers a convenient explanation for the unfortunate things that happen to people in the course of their lifetimes without attaching blame to anyone, except of course, the bugbear. Mental institutions and morgues, Jimmy observes, are filled with bugbear-deficient people.

Jimmy's bugbear is his uncle Jimmy, whom Jimmy privately calls U.J. According to Annette, Uncle Jimmy is a cousin of Jimmy's father. Years ago, when Jimmy was a ten-year-old whiz kid and such things were of interest to him, he had once asked Annette for more precise genealogical information, but his mother had only shrugged and said, "It's no big deal. Go ask him yourself." Jimmy has never done this, mostly because his uncle is out of town a lot, and when he does show up, he intimidates Jimmy by glancing (either menacingly or conde-scendingly, Jimmy thinks) at him out of the corners of his eyes. Later, when Jimmy had needed a copy of his birth certificate for the university admissions office, he had asked Annette for it.

"Uncle Jimmy has it, and all other papers."

"Why does he keep our papers?"

"It's no big deal."

"It's not right."

"He is the man of the family. Chinese custom from the old country. The man, oldest man, father, uncle, cousin, brother, keeps the documents. It's no big deal."

After Jimmy had insisted that he was perfectly capable of taking care of any official papers relating to himself, his mother and sisters, Annette had retrieved them.

When Jimmy had looked at his birth certificate, he had been horrified to discover his father's name was James Sung. Jimmy couldn't remember if Annette had ever told him his father's Christian name, but in any case, Annette's fund of information about his progenitor had always been rather vague. Several versions of his father's death had been supplied when he was younger. In one, Jimmy's father was swept off a fishing boat into the Gulf of Alaska; in another, he was crushed by a falling tree somewhere near Telegraph Creek; a third had him succumbing to a virulent disease contracted at a gold mine near Yellowknife. When Jimmy had finally got up the nerve, as a cocky young teenager, to point out the discrepancies, Annette had told him she didn't know the exact cause of death, just that he had died somewhere in the north while working hard to support his family. "Anyway, it doesn't matter. Dead is dead, right?"

Inevitably the day had arrived when Jimmy, too, acknow-ledged the impeccable logic of Dead is dead.

Still, Jimmy had thought it more than a little odd that his father and his uncle should have the same name.

"No big deal," says Annette. "In the old country the health conditions weren't so good, many children didn't live to grow up. A father often gave his name to the first two sons, or even three or four sons, so chances are increased that his name will continue on."

Lucille, who had been listening, poked her tongue out at Jimmy and teased him for wanting to be the only James Sung in the world. When Lucille behaved like this, Jimmy was at a loss to comprehend how his mother and father could have committed the gross error of bringing a child like her into the world; he concluded, however, he could not do much to reverse the process now, except perhaps to forswear any opportunity he himself might have to father more Sung children.

Of course that was years ago, and nowadays Jimmy's position has modified somewhat. His precarious financial situation has caused him to admit (but only to himself) that he would be fortunate indeed if he could find a single individual of the opposite sex to agree to collaborate with him in the production of a child. Jimmy finds this circumstance especially galling whenever he considers the disparity between his income and that of Uncle Jimmy.

For as long as Jimmy can remember, Annette has worked seven days a week. Once when Jimmy had suggested that Uncle Jimmy might be prepared to help out, Annette had informed him coldly that she wanted nothing from anyone else, and that included Uncle Jimmy. Understandably, then, Jimmy had been surprised when he learned Annette paid no rent for their house on Union Street, nor for the commercial property they occupied on East Pender. When queried about Uncle Jimmy's role in all this, Annette said her arrangements with his uncle were none of Jimmy's business.

In any event, Jimmy had no legitimate right to complain about his uncle's reluctance to share his wealth, since Jimmy and his sisters, so said Annette, were stuck way off in some remote branch of the Sung family tree (Jimmy made the comparison of the sun and its planets being located in the outer reaches of the Milky Way, far removed from the galaxy's heart) while Uncle Jimmy was a direct descendant of the first Sung who arrived in British Columbia with the primary wave of gold seekers from California. This illustrious ancestor had settled near Burrard Inlet, building shacks that he leased to transients, thus demonstrating that the first Canadian Sung knew more about laying down the foundation of a family fortune than the gold-crazed diggers from California. He had cohabited with a native Indian woman and through his connection with her had acquired ownership of several blocks of land that later became part of the port and city of Vancouver. It makes sense, then, that Jimmy has concluded the only benefit he is likely to enjoy from his Sung connection is that some day (when?) his distant relationship to his uncle will nudge him a little further along the torturous ascent to the pinnacle of legal fame and fortune.

But wait! There is something else: as a child, Jimmy remembers Annette saying that because Uncle Jimmy never married, the tangled web of Sung inter-family relationships offered a possibility Jimmy might end up as one of his uncle's heirs. Nowadays, though, Jimmy's age and experience of real life have separated him from the vague hints once thrown out by his mother. Besides, on the occasions when his uncle visits his mother's store and takes the trouble to climb the twenty stairs to view Jimmy diligently slaving away in his dreary little legal domain, it is all too obvious to Jimmy that this aging man does not particularly like him and has no plans to bequeath him a cent of cash. Still, Jimmy does not blame Annette for arousing his childish ambitions. He excuses her overly optimistic words as the natural, spontaneous expression of a doting young mother, and besides, albeit inadvertently, she has provided him with his own bugbear, namely, Uncle Jimmy.

On this evening, Jimmy sits reading a spy novel in the Sungs' small, over-furnished living room and mingles his thoughts and emotions with those of the characters in the story. Jimmy believes he would make an excellent spy and regrets the improbability of ever being given an opportunity to display his inborn talent for intrigue. Later, before getting into his narrow bed, Jimmy strips off his clothes and stares at himself in the mirror set into the back of his bedroom door. He wonders what will eventually happen to the person whose image he sees reflected there.

Jimmy has never regarded himself as particularly attractive looking—and there's the mirror with confirmation. He turns sideways to observe the curved body part at the base of his flat belly, which he has been putting to good use for a few years now in once-a-week sessions with a woman named Evelyn Chan. Jimmy had guided her late husband's will through probate. Following settlement of the estate the widow had asked Jimmy to assist her in purchasing a townhouse. While Jimmy was arranging the deal, she had let him know she had been married to an impotent old man and now intended to enjoy life. She had then invited Jimmy to become a participant in her pleasurable activities.

Until he met Evelyn Chan Jimmy had thought of sex as a complement to love, and even today, he finds it difficult to believe what goes on between them is accomplished so dispassionately. She is always the dominant partner in their physical encounters, but why should Jimmy object to remaining supine while his amorous partner straddles him? Furthermore, as Jimmy frequently reminds himself, his supine position enables him to observe the changes that occur in Evelyn Chan's face and body. He enjoys holding her hips and anticipating the moment when she trembles and moans before collapsing onto him. Then it's his turn. This performance will be repeated twice during the hour and a half Jimmy spends with the widow, and Jimmy's only quibble is that his visits are restricted to one a week, which leads him to conclude he is not alone in enjoying the widow's company. To offset this disappointment, Jimmy consoles himself with the knowledge that only a tiny number of young men in dubious financial circumstances similar to his own have been as fortunate as he in being selected to lie alongside, or rather under, such an enthusiastic partner as Evelyn Chan.

But now, as Jimmy stands looking into the mirror, he remembers how Janet MacDougail crossed her legs, and allows his imagination to take a closer look. And, instantaneously, there in the mirror is a serious erection. Feeling guilty, Jimmy tries to think of something that will change his mood, like the kind of food Caucasians eat. Even that doesn't work. Jimmy sighs, turns off the light and gets into bed.

The following morning he sits in his office, reading a five-page letter from a client attempting to make the point that because Jimmy has failed to locate his missing wife, the client is under no obligation to pay him. How is Jimmy to know that as he now wades through this indignant epistle the client's spouse is thoroughly enjoying herself more than two thousand kilometres away in a draw-off on the Alaska Highway. At the exact moment Jimmy comes to the end of the husband's letter, she is scuttling from beneath the body of the driver of a semi to replace her underpants and settle down for a well-deserved nap in the coziness of the trailer cab. The driver knows nothing about this woman other than her first name, and plans to discard her in Whitehorse. He figures she will do well for herself in the Yukon.

As Jimmy begins drafting his reply, the phone rings and he responds to the call with a crisp "Sung Investigations and Law Office. James Sung speaking." A male voice curtly asks when it will be convenient for Mr. Sung to call on Mrs. Charles J. MacDougail. Jimmy, after rustling papers close to the telephone and pretending to consult an appointment book, informs the voice he can just manage to squeeze in a brief visit at eleven o'clock that same morning.

Jimmy is an on-time fanatic, and he drives Annette's car into the MacDougail driveway three minutes before eleven. The house, while it cannot be described as a mansion, is pretentious enough to need a black-suited man to open the embossed front door, thus affording Jimmy the opportunity to make a dignified entry into the spacious hall. "Mrs. MacDougail is expecting you, sir," the black-suited man informs Jimmy, and precedes him into a long room where a woman sits beside some French windows. "Mr. Sung," the man announces, leaving Jimmy to find his way through clusters of tapestry-covered chairs and sofas and dark, highly polished tables holding a litter of lamps, bowls and porcelain figurines.

Mrs. MacDougail, who is laboriously implanting stitches into a piece of canvas, doesn't look up when Jimmy coughs to announce his presence. Jimmy imagines himself having a heart attack in the room, during which Mrs. MacDougail remains indifferent, merely pressing an invisible button on the floor with her foot to call the black-suited man back to remove the body, without once having ceased to draw the thread in and out of the canvas.

"I understand my granddaughter visited your office yesterday. Is that correct, Mr. Sung?" she eventually says.

"She did. I advised her to discuss our meeting with you." Jimmy feels anger rising because Mrs. MacDougail does not invite him to sit but keeps him standing, like a servant.

"It's a pity Janet didn't speak to me before seeing you." She seems to crouch in her chair, and her voluminous purple-and-red gown spreads over her large-framed, overweight body. He is shocked when he notices she is careless about details of her dress. Several buttons on the bodice of the gown are unfastened, revealing underclothes and sagging flesh. What Jimmy sees makes him uneasy since it raises in his mind the spectre of his beloved mother becoming careless in personal matters as old age encroaches upon her—he can hardly bear to contemplate that such a thing might happen.

"Mrs. MacDougail, I really can't afford to waste valuable time travelling across town only to be told you wish to veto Janet's expressed wishes for an investigation."

"That is not my meaning, Mr. Sung," she responds haughtily. "My view is simply that Janet should have raised any questions she might have about her brother's death with me first before contacting you." She raises the canvas and examines it. "Have you formed an opinion based on what Janet told you?"

"Not yet." Jimmy has no intention of supplying Mrs. MacDougail with any ideas free of charge.

"Unfortunately Janet finds it hard to accept what happened to Martin. Is that your impression, Mr. Sung?"

"More or less."

"Which is quite understandable in a girl who thought so

highly of her brother. What did Janet actually tell you, Mr. Sung?"

"I'm sure you realize information provided by a client is confidential," Jimmy replies with his best business smile.

"My granddaughter is not your client," Mrs. MacDougail points out.

"If that is so, I'm not obliged to tell you anything, Mrs. MacDougail."

"But what could Janet have possibly told you? What does she actually know? The facts are these: Martin drove to Stanley Park, left his car there and then walked onto the Lions Gate Bridge." Jimmy watches as Mrs. MacDougail snips and removes green thread from her needle and rethreads it with a strand of red, finding it all quite nerve-racking. "Martin had been out the night before, attending a social gathering . . ." Mrs. MacDougail pauses to complete threading her needle. ". . . and the people there informed the police Martin seemed unusually excited, that he wasn't himself. I assume Janet explained all this." Jimmy nods. "It's really quite clear and straightforward, Mr. Sung." Jimmy nods again. Mrs. MacDougail looks up, and Jimmy is surprised to see how closely she resembles her granddaughter. Although her dark skin is lined and mottled, her neck heavy with fat, behind these blemishes of age he can discern the strong facial structure of the girl who sat in his office the previous afternoon. "I don't want Janet fretting over her brother's death."

"I'd like to know exactly what you expect from me, Mrs. MacDougail," Jimmy says.

"I am hoping we can set Janet's mind at rest, Mr. Sung. I want you to convince her the police have uncovered the truth about her brother's death and there's nothing more she can do."

Jimmy counts to thirty before replying. "Let's be open with each other, Mrs. MacDougail. You are prepared to provide money for an investigation, but only on condition I reach the same conclusion as the police. Is this correct?"

"You have misunderstood, Mr. Sung. You will examine the evidence, and based on that evidence you will reach the only *possible* conclusion."

"No, Mrs. MacDougail," Jimmy says, deciding to take charge. "Given the facts we know, at least four different conclusions can be reached." He ticks them off on his fingers. "One, Martin jumped from the bridge; two, he accidentally fell from the bridge; three, he was thrown off while alive; and four, he was killed elsewhere and dropped from the bridge afterwards."

"I am not interested in conjecture, Mr. Sung. I'm only interested in having Janet—"

"But suppose for argument's sake that evidence is uncovered that substantiates Janet's belief. What then?"

By now Mrs. MacDougail has become so impatient she accidentally jabs the needle into her finger. "Damnation!" she exclaims. "Mr. Sung, I didn't bring you here to find any new evidence. And you'll be paid well to make sure there is none. Is that understood?"

"I don't question your desire to provide Janet with an acceptable explanation of her brother's death. In fact, I sympathize with you. But I have an obligation—"

"The only obligation you have is to protect the interests of your client."

"But I can't rule out other possible explanations of Martin's death. Surely you must see that, Mrs. MacDougail."

"Mr. Sung . . . Martin killed himself."

"I'm sorry, Mrs. MacDougail, but I can't agree to undertake an investigation and be restricted in what I can and can't do." Jimmy turns and prepares to make his exit.

"One moment," she says. Jimmy turns back to face her. "Mr. Sung, I am not asking you to mislead Janet. All I ask is that you confirm what the police have told us so Janet can come to terms with what's happened to her brother. Now, is that too much to ask?"

Jimmy pulls up a chair and sits facing her. "But what if the evidence doesn't confirm the finding of suicide?"

"Someone told me you are an intelligent young man, and I would hope you have sufficient sense not to allow such a thing to happen, Mr. Sung."

"And who told you that, Mrs. MacDougail?"

"It doesn't matter. Now, either you will do this or you will not. So tell me, which is it?"

Jimmy hesitates, realizing that in presenting her ultimatum Mrs. MacDougail has regained the upper hand. "I'm sure you appreciate that a great many things may have been going on in Martin's life that you knew nothing about."

"Martin had no reason to lie to me."

"That may be true. But he may have omitted to inform you about some of his activities, things you might not have approved of."

"You are in no position to draw conclusions about what Martin either said or did not say to me, Mr. Sung. Or are you assessing Martin's honesty based on your own experience?"

"I consider myself to be as honest as most people." Modesty prevents Jimmy from proclaiming that he truly believes himself to be a lot more honest than most people, except for Annette, and there are a couple of things about her that occasionally trouble him.

"That's no great recommendation," Mrs. MacDougail sneers, and Jimmy flushes. "I've no doubt you lie when it serves your purpose to do so."

They stare at each other, mutual dislike flowing across the space separating them. Mrs. MacDougail looks down at the canvas on which she is embroidering a spray of red roses. "My granddaughter has requested your assistance. That being so, I hope you will follow my suggestion and use discretion. Send me the bill for your services. And don't pad it."

Jimmy forces himself to ignore this outright insult. Instead, he determinedly lays out what he plans to do. "We agree that I will undertake an investigation into your grandson's death, and while it is unlikely new evidence will be forthcoming that contradicts conclusions already reached by the police, nevertheless I retain the right, should I uncover new evidence, to communicate it to the authorities."

"I don't know how old you are, Mr. Sung, but you're far too young to behave so pompously." With no comeback handy, Jimmy bows slightly in the general direction of Mrs. MacDougail and makes for the doorway, aware he is behaving like a fool and needs only a pince-nez to convey an impression of total asininity. He is about to move into the hall when Mrs. MacDougail says, "I must tell you, Mr. Sung, that Janet neither saw nor spoke with her brother the night before he died. She could not have done so, because she was out all that day with me, and Martin did not come to the house in the evening. I should also tell you that because Janet thought a lot of her brother she tended to overlook some of his . . . limitations."

While driving back to the office, Jimmy tells himself his behaviour throughout the interview was correct in every detail, each point he raised was valid and succinctly presented. Yet he remains vaguely uneasy with his performance; he senses that even the most sensible point of view when offered by a younger, less experienced person to someone older can easily be transformed by the recipient into a fool's babble. But it is possible that were Jimmy pickled in the brine of experience and not so pleased with the way he has handled Mrs. MacDougail, he would have listened more carefully to what she told him and have withdrawn immediately from the investigation. But Jimmy does not do this because pride has replaced sound judgment. He tells himself he will succeed in uncovering the truth about Martin MacDougail, even if it means liberating pain-filled ghosts from the MacDougail family closet; while he may be vaguely uneasy about his own performance, he is determined that no one (especially a rich, snobbish harridan) will gainsay him.

Jimmy goes to his office and chews over the information he has gathered about the MacDougail family. When the telephone rings, he guesses who it is before he raises the receiver.

"Gran says it's all right for you to start working. Isn't that exciting?"

Jimmy agrees it is, and then asks Janet what she knows about her brother's friends. "Did he ever speak to you about them?"

"Yes, sometimes."

"I want you to make a list of the names you remember and mail it to me. Will you do that for me, Janet?"

"I suppose I could." She abruptly hangs up and Jimmy, after staring at the telephone as if it is responsible, replaces it in its cradle. Sighing, he leaves his office and goes down into the store to assemble the day's takings. These he seals in an envelope before walking down the street and slipping them into the depository chute of Annette's bank. This self-imposed regime had begun one afternoon when Jimmy, standing by his office window, had spotted Lucille meandering along the street, idly swinging an envelope containing Annette's receipts for the day, being followed by two men. Jimmy had immediately abandoned his position at the window and raced down the stairs to rescue Lucille from—so Jimmy surmised—an attempted robbery. When he reached the street there was no sign of either Lucille or the men, and Jimmy was convinced his sister was being carried off to a back alley where the men were going to rip off her clothes and, after doing unmentionable things to her beautiful body, cast it into a nearby dumpster before running off to spend Annette's laboriously earned money on drugs and booze. Jimmy had run backward and forward on the street, and on his third pass beheld Lucille emerging from Mrs. Liu's dress shop where she had been looking at the latest fashions. At almost the same moment he spotted the two men sitting at a table inside the window of Lee's Cafe, quietly drinking coffee. Afterwards when he had delivered a lecture to Lucille on how vital it was to transport Annette's money rapidly from the store to the bank, Lucille had told him if he thought the job was so terribly important, then he could do it himself. And that is exactly what Jimmy has done to this day.

Early Saturday morning Jimmy telephones police headquarters and, following the usual delays and runarounds, is informed that a Sergeant Robson is in charge of the Martin MacDougail case but is off duty until Monday. Just as Jimmy is terminating this unpromising conversation, the office door opens and in strolls his bugbear.

As usual, the moment his uncle enters his office Jimmy becomes acutely aware of his own inadequacies. Today Jimmy is casually dressed in jeans, open-necked shirt and a light sweater, whereas his uncle is immaculately clad in a fawn-coloured suit, including a waistcoat, which tends toward being slightly "horsey" in style and cut. There is a valid reason for the equestrian look: Uncle Jimmy is a member of that select club which governs horseracing in and around Vancouver; furthermore, he holds an honorary position in the organization that allows him to supervise the collection of horse urine following each race sponsored by the club.

Although Jimmy has never made much of the fact, there is a physical resemblance between himself and his uncle, especially in their thin, elongated faces and slender bodies. But Jimmy is much taller than his uncle, an advantage that Jimmy now seeks to minimize by sinking as far as possible into his chair. He has no idea why his uncle has come, but suspects Annette has telephoned him in order to make inquiries about the MacDougail family. One of the oddities about the relationship between his family and his uncle is that Uncle Jimmy and Annette talk on the telephone every day if he is in North America, and every other day if he is abroad. Once, when Jimmy asked Annette about this, she waved a hand and said, "Oh, your uncle just likes to keep in touch. It's no big deal."

Uncle Jimmy now stands in front of his nephew's desk, eyeing him. "Hello, Nephew," he says, "what are you up to these days?"

"The usual," Jimmy mumbles.

"Hm . . . ." his uncle comments. "Has your income risen above the poverty line yet?" Jimmy mutters he's not doing too badly. "Hm . . . ." repeats Uncle Jimmy. The noncommittal sound his uncle makes causes anxiety to grip Jimmy, and even the dust-edged diplomas hanging on the wall seem to wilt and lose some of their distinction. His uncle explains that he is off to Abbotsford with Sam Mackintosh to look over a couple of colts. Jimmy has heard this gambit before and wonders why his uncle continues to use it because, while it is true his uncle puts in a lot of time at the race track during the season, he has never placed a bet on a horse, much less owned one. The gambling is all done by Sam Mackintosh. Jimmy once asked Annette why Uncle Jimmy went around Vancouver accompanied by a man whose sole interests in life are gambling and alcohol. Annette's explanation was simple; his uncle owes a life-long debt to Sam Mackintosh.

The story goes something like this: a young, wealthy and immensely conceited Uncle Jimmy drives to English Bay in the company of a young woman he wishes to impress before seducing. That same day Sam is sitting in an elevated chair on the beach, life-guarding. Uncle Jimmy, who possesses more vanity than swimming prowess, trails the woman into the water and follows her as she churns out into the bay. By the time the woman has begun swimming back to shore, Uncle Jimmy is exhausted and in imminent danger of disappearing beneath the surface. Fortunately Sam sees that Uncle Jimmy is in trouble and slices through the waves at twice the woman's speed, drags Uncle Jimmy back to the beach, thumps his back to expel water from his lungs, then dumps him onto a blanket beside the young woman, who is now sunning her broad, muscular back. Uncle Jimmy recovers his wits, drops the girl and forms a friendship with Sam Mackintosh, while the latter forthwith abandons any attempt to earn a living and takes to spending Uncle Jimmy's money on booze and racehorses that invariably finish out of the money. Annette ends the life-saving saga with this admonishment: "Don't ever speak ill of Sam Mackintosh to your uncle. Sam Mackintosh saved your uncle's life and he's never forgotten it." As a child, Jimmy found it impossible to imagine his uncle would ever express gratitude to anybody, but has come to understand that the relationship between the two men is based on a life-contract Uncle Jimmy honours to this day. Still, understanding the reason for his uncle's tolerance of Sam Mackintosh does not prevent Jimmy from wishing from time to time that Uncle Jimmy had sunk to the bottom of English Bay.

"I hear you're doing work for the MacDougail family," his uncle says. Jimmy nods and asks if his uncle knows any of the family. "I knew one of Margaret MacDougail's sons casually," his uncle replies. "He spent a lot of time on his yacht. As a matter of fact I believe he—and his wife too—died in a boating accident. Well, it's time I was on my way. Sam'll be wondering what happened to me. I'll leave you to your arduous labours, Nephew." Although Jimmy always reminds himself these chats with his uncle consist of little more than small talk, nevertheless he is unable to alter the distorted image of the older man he has created over the years. Consequently he searches his uncle's remarks for hidden implications and deep meanings. The end result of this chat is that after Uncle Jimmy leaves, instead of driving out to UBC to contact people who may have known Martin MacDougail, Jimmy dawdles the afternoon away, drawing up lists of things to do. When he realizes how much time he has wasted he sighs, walks to the window, looks down into the street, and on the pavement immediately below him sees Janet MacDougail, laughing and talking with Lucille.

Jimmy's immediate reaction is one of intense jealousy. How dare Lucille prevent Janet from hurrying up the stairs to see him! He moves back to the desk, arranges himself and waits. After several minutes he returns to the window to find them still preoccupied with their pointless (he is positive of this) chatter. The sight infuriates him and he returns to his desk where he types a letter to Mrs. MacDougail, informing her that after careful consideration he has decided not to proceed with the investigation of her grandson's death. When he hears the downstairs door open, he rips the paper from the machine, tears up the letter, composes himself and waits, confident he will hear Janet's footsteps as she runs up the stairs to see him. But instead he hears Lucille call his name and then say, "He's gone," before closing the door. Jimmy is angry with himself for not having gone down to separate Janet from Lucille—and furious with Lucille for thinking she can take over a client. He locks up and returns to Union Street, determined to tell Lucille he will not tolerate her poking her nose into his business. He goes into the kitchen, glares at Annette, who is preparing the evening meal, and hears voices issuing from the seldom-used dining room. He looks into the room and sees Janet MacDougail, placidly helping Lucille set the table for dinner. Janet smiles at him, and at that moment butterflies are let loose in his stomach, his knees become jelly and Jimmy falls in love.

The realization of what has happened shocks Jimmy, although he retains sufficient objectivity to grasp there is little he can do now to reverse the process, which is, he reflects, something like jumping off a cliff—there is no in-between, you either do or you don't. If you do, you walk across the room and invite the person with whom you have fallen in love to sit beside you in order that you can show her how to arrange chopsticks in her fingers, all the while aware of your mother hovering nearby, thinking at last she has found a potential wife for you.

Annette's delight in Janet's presence in her home is so apparent it embarrasses Jimmy, although Janet seems oblivious. (Naturally Annette would have preferred a hard-working young woman of Chinese ancestry for Jimmy, but being a pragmatist, she is prepared to compromise, provided the object of Jimmy's affections has the right social connections and plenty of money.) Jimmy thinks maybe Janet views Annette as a poor but kind-hearted ethnic who ekes out a meagre existence in the nether regions of the city, and given any other circumstance would be furious that anyone might consider herself superior to his mother; but any anger Jimmy might feel on hearing Janet's opinion of his mother, should she choose to express one, would in any event immediately evaporate in the cloud of scented warmth that envelopes him as he sits close beside his newly discovered love. Although he tries to avoid it, he cannot help himself from seeing an image reflected in Annette's eyes of Janet and him in one of the gardens at Queen Elizabeth Park, posing for their wedding picture. Has he, Jimmy asks himself, endured years of intellectual discipline, ingesting English common law, the Napoleonic Code, and Canadian criminal jurisprudence in order to end up sitting at his mother's dining-room table while she mentally marries him off to someone who, for all she knows, still sucks her thumb in bed at night?

In the middle of the meal Julie appears with her three-year-old twin daughters, Anna and Alice. Judging from Janet's indifference to them, Jimmy concludes Janet's maternal drive is not very strong—either that, or it has not yet made an appearance. Immediately after supper Lucille takes Janet up to her bedroom, where Jimmy supposes they examine Lucille's wardrobe and listen to records. (Over the years Jimmy has periodically attempted to elevate Lucille's taste in music by taking her to an occasional symphony concert and to the annual Christmas sing-along performance of *The Messiah*. "Thank goodness that's over," Lucille invariably says when each piece in the musical program terminates, adding while at the same time yawning and sighing, "How much longer before we can go home?" If Jimmy did not adore Lucille, he would probably whack her over the head with the program notes, but as it is, he continues to excuse Lucille's musical ignorance and prays she will never meet one of his music-loving clients. Never mind that so far Jimmy has not encountered such a client; but he remains ever hopeful the day will come when a cultured client asks his opinion of a musical performance. To this end, he carefully peruses what music critics in Vancouver newspapers have to say and prepares suitable conversational tidbits such as "I thought the strings lacked finesse" and "The brass had a bad evening, particularly the French horns." Why is it that those of his clients given to chitchat prefer to talk hockey and baseball?

While Janet and Lucille are upstairs, Julie informs Jimmy there is nothing wrong with girls marrying and having babies when they are young, provided they are ready for it. She picks up the twins and dumps them into Jimmy's lap. Julie is the kind of person who believes if only other people had what she has (her twins, a variety store, and Bill Wong), then perforce they will be as happy as she. Jimmy grimaces but says nothing, knowing it is a waste of time to tell Julie she is barking up the wrong tree.

While Jimmy waits to drive Janet home in the Corolla, he hears her arrange with Lucille to spend the following weekend at the MacDougail house.

As they walk to the car Janet tells Jimmy she thinks Lucille is a very nice person. "So are your mother and Julie. Sometimes I feel I never really had any parents." Jimmy opens the car door for Janet, irritated with himself for doing this because he never extends the courtesy to anybody else, even Annette. He wonders if his politeness indicates a peon-like attitude on his part and resolves forthwith never to open a car door for Janet again, while at the back of his mind aware he will do so if given the opportunity.

"Well, you have a grandmother."

"It's not the same as having a mother around all the time. Although Gran is good to me. Is your father away a lot?"

"He's dead."

"Like mine. Do you remember much about him?"

"Nothing."

Janet lies back in the seat and looks up at the car roof. "It's funny how a person can forget horrible things. You think you'll never forget them. But you do."

"What sorts of things?" Janet does not respond, but turns her head, looks out of the car window and asks which way they are going home. "Through Queen Elizabeth Park. It's on the way, and I thought we could walk around a bit. We'll have time before it gets dark. I have a couple of things I want to discuss with you—after you finish telling me about the horrible things that have happened to you."

He feels that Janet is looking closely at him as he drives up the hill, looking for a place to park. "There's nothing to tell," she eventually says, as he pulls into an empty slot and turns off the motor.

As they stroll toward the gardens, she slips her arm through Jimmy's as if it is the most natural thing in the world to do. They stand near the viewing telescopes and look out over the city towards the mountains on the North Shore and those that soar in the east, compressing the Fraser River into an immense, tumultuous gorge. Jimmy becomes acutely aware of his contact with Janet's right shoulder and hip. "My mother and sisters are very family-oriented," he begins.

"Can we see where you live from here?" she asks, and Jimmy vaguely points to an area in the grid below them. "It's about there," he says, and continues. "Mother believes no man can be successful in life unless he has a wife." He glances at Janet's face and sees an expression similar to the one that appears on the faces of small children as they listen to their teachers explaining something beyond their comprehension. Jimmy decides to defer telling Janet about Annette's plans to marry him off to a more propitious moment in their conversation. Instead he asks her if she has made a list of her brother's friends for him.

She burrows into her shoulder bag and finally brings out a much-folded piece of lined paper, which Jimmy takes and examines. The writing is childish, and surnames and addresses are missing. "These are the only names I ever heard Martin use," she explains.

"It's a start, anyway," Jimmy says, thinking the list is close to being useless. "Shall we walk around the garden?" They pace the crest of the hill, following the curve of the observatory dome, then descend into the old quarry, now transformed into a spectacular garden.

"Do you like flowers?" she asks as they halt beside a flower bed carpeted with yellow and purple pansies.

"I enjoy looking at flowers, but I don't know much about them," Jimmy answers and decides to risk carrying on with his earlier discussion. "My mother and sisters are almost fanatic about finding me a wife."

"How odd," she comments. "I thought men found wives for themselves."

"Most do," Jimmy says, as they move on to look at the azaleas. "And I'd prefer to do it that way too. But my mother and sisters regard every unmarried young woman they meet as a prospective wife for me." When Janet moves her arm away from his, stops, and looks at him, he realizes she is beginning to understand what he has been trying to tell her.

"You mean . . ?" Her mouth is open wide enough for Jimmy to see several expensive gold inlays in her molars. (Jimmy has often come across passages in novels where young women gasp for any number of reasons ranging from horror at the intentions of ghastly maniacs to enjoyment of illicit sexual coupling on creaky motel beds. He is surprised at finding life imitating a literary cliche.)

"Well . . ." Jimmy blunders on, ". . . you're beautiful. And . . . well . . . you're healthy . . . and . . ." He stops—he has suddenly run up against the barrier of Janet MacDougail's wealth.

The effect on Janet is not what Jimmy expects. He is prepared for laughter, even for imperious rejection; but not for blushes and tear-filled eyes. "Oh . . . I thought . . . maybe . . . they liked me for . . . myself," she whispers.

"Oh, but they do, they do," Jimmy takes her hand and pats it. "But they can't separate finding me a wife from just liking a person. I mean . . . Look . . ." He realizes he is making things worse and makes a stab at being humorous. "Why, in the past year alone, Mother's come up with at least three dozen possible wives. She can't help herself . . . she's on the lookout twenty-four hours a day. Well . . . I'm exaggerating things a bit . . . but you see what I'm getting at, don't you?" Looking at Janet's puzzled expression, Jimmy observes she does not understand at all and tries again. "Janet, it's nothing to get upset about. I was only trying to clear up any possible misunderstanding that might arise."

"You mean you wouldn't consider marrying me, is that what you're trying to say?"

"No, no, of course not. I mean, that's not the point. The reason I'm telling you all this . . . I mean . . . if circumstances were different . . . I . . . ." By this time Jimmy has no idea what he is saying. What he wants is to stop the tears sliding from Janet's eyes and running down her cheeks. He wants to find the right words to comfort her, but doesn't know what they are. "I mean . . . I'm sure you'd make a wonderful wife . . . a perfect wife . . . and if things were different . . . I mean . . . I like you a lot . . . in fact . . . I know it seems utterly ridiculous . . . but . . . I think . . . I've fallen in love with you." And there Jimmy abruptly stops, aware his behaviour is incredibly gauche. Yet he knows he must continue. Like someone who steps onto a sheet of ice and finds himself cascading down the side of a mountain, he has no choice. "I just wanted you to know that when my mother and sisters start telling you what a great guy I am . . . that it's . . . well . . . not altogether true . . . I mean . . . I'm not a bad sort, but . . . Look, the last thing I want is to upset you. Come on, please. Let's go on." He pats her hand. "Please."

Janet once more slips her arm through his and they proceed, matching their stride and winding in silence along paths taking them past rhododendron bushes whose glistening heads bob as though demanding their attention. At last they stop beside a bed of riotously coloured tulips, and Janet sighs. "I'm sure you'd make a nice husband, Jimmy. But I couldn't think of marrying you . . . or anyone. I haven't even started university yet. Though I could think about it after I graduate. But I expect you'll already be married by then."

"I doubt it," Jimmy mutters, as they move through a cloud of intoxicating lilac scent.

"Still, it was nice of you to be honest with me about your mother," Janet says. "I do trust you."

"Thank you," Jimmy says, "and don't worry too much about Mother; most parents are like her." He is surprised that Janet has ignored his declaration of love, but concludes it was lost somewhere in his incoherent babble.

"I suppose. Of course, I haven't got a mother organizing me. I just have Gran."

"Well, I'm glad that's cleared up," Jimmy says, in a hearty scout-master voice.

"Oh yes, I'm glad too," Janet agrees. "Let's walk some more, shall we?"

They continue to follow the perimeter of the park, occa-sionally halting to look at flowering bushes or admire another vista of the city. Jimmy is acutely aware that his promenade with Janet is the first time he has actually been for a walk with a young woman other than Lucille or Julie. (In his adolescent years and while at university, Jimmy was so committed to being a whiz kid he rarely thought of girls and never imagined a young woman might walk beside him one day, her arm through his, her hand resting lightly on his wrist.)

Janet regains her good spirits and talks about herself. She tells Jimmy she loves riding in sports cars and hopes to learn to drive her brother's car, now sitting unused in the garage.

"You're sure your brother came to see you the night before he died? You're positive he promised you a ride in his new car on the same day he died?" Jimmy asks.

"Quite sure."

"What else did you do that day?"

"Gran took me shopping. I saw Martin after we came back."

"Do you remember what time it was?"

"I don't know . . . after dinner."

"Did you speak to your grandmother after Martin's visit?"

"I expect I went downstairs to say goodnight."

"You didn't tell your grandmother you'd seen Martin?"

"No."

"Why not?"

"Because she'd have wanted to know whether Martin was drinking . . . and stuff like that."

"Did anybody else in the house see Martin?"

"I don't know. He came to my room and told me he'd take me for a ride the next day, then he left. Why are you asking me these questions?"

"I want to know where Martin went that Saturday . . . and what he did."

"He was probably just hanging out. That's mostly what he did."

"He told you that?"

"No . . . but I knew. He hated university, he was always cutting classes. He wouldn't have been there at all, except Gran insisted. And I know Gran's going to make me go too. I don't know why, I've never said I want to."

"So. Martin came to your room, stayed a short while, then left. And that was the last time you saw him?"

She agrees, then asks if they can talk about something else. Jimmy suggests she tell him more about herself, and she immediately reels off a list of activities that includes swimming, though, she explains, she hates being on the school swim team because the coach puts her in relay races where she is expected to overtake swimmers already a pool-length ahead of her. "They always team me with the slowest swimmers," she complains. "And that's not fair because if I don't catch up, the coach gets mad at me and says I could have won if I had tried harder."

"Could you?" Jimmy asks.

"Maybe. Our coach said I could be on a national team if I worked at it. But I'd have to practise a lot." She laughs and presses Jimmy's arm against her side. "Martin hated it when I beat him. I never liked racing him, but he'd say 'Race you to the other end of the pool, Jan,' then when I got there first, he'd get mad. Maybe that's why I don't like being on the swim team."

"Did Martin drink much?"

"I suppose so. People do, don't they? Do you drink?"

"A bit. Was Martin drinking that Saturday night?"

"I guess . . ."

"Why did Martin have his own apartment?"

"To escape from Gran."

"When he came to visit you, did he talk about what he was doing?"

"Sometimes. But mostly he came when he was feeling depressed . . . though if I asked what was wrong he always said I wouldn't understand."

"Do you think you would have?"

"Maybe. It usually had to do with his girlfriends. They'd get mad at him when he didn't show up for dates. Sometimes they even phoned the house."

"Why would they do that when Martin had his own phone?"

"I guess because he was hardly ever at his apartment. I tried to get him to be nicer to his girlfriends."

"What did he say?"

"He called me a stupid little idiot." Jimmy sees that Janet is chewing at her lower lip. "Martin told me you can buy girls like you buy things at a store. All you needed was the money."

"He was probably exaggerating. Do you know how much allowance he got from your grandmother?"

"Oh, our money doesn't come from Gran. It's from the trust. I get money from it too, but Gran looks after it for me." She is silent for a moment, then asks, "Do you think I'm stupid?"

"Anything but," Jimmy reassures her. "You seem very sensible to me."

"Maybe I am, but I'm not really smart like some girls in my class. They're good at math and science and I'm not." She sighs, and for a moment Jimmy feels the curve of her hidden breast touch his arm. The brief contact thrills him far more than touching the naked breasts of Evelyn Chan. "When Martin was still alive, I was supposed to be just a girl who didn't know very much. But now I want to try and act more grown-up."

"Why? Isn't it better for you just to be yourself?"

"But I might say or do something silly . . . and then people would laugh at me."

"Don't let that worry you. Everyone says silly things," says Jimmy, who once, at age twelve, had flattered himself he had completely eradicated all foolish thought and behaviour from his life. He consults his watch. "It's getting late. Your grandmother is probably wondering where you are."

"She knows I'm with you."

Still, they turn and go back to the car. Jimmy opens the car door for Janet, but instead of getting in she stands by the door, nibbling her lip. "Were you serious? You know . . . about liking me . . . and about your mother and sisters looking for a wife for you?" she finally asks.

"Quite serious," Jimmy solemnly replies. "But remember, they asked you to stay for dinner because they like you."

"Do you think Lucille really and truly likes me?"

"I'm sure of it. She took you up to her bedroom. She never allows me in there."

Janet smiles. "I feel the same way about my bedroom, too . . . though I don't suppose anybody would want to come into it." Jimmy almost blurts, I would! I would! "Martin just used to barge in whenever he felt like it." Her expression changes and Jimmy perceives something akin to desperation. "You weren't offended, were you . . . you know . . . when I said I couldn't think of marrying you? Gran says it's ridiculous for a girl my age to even have a boyfriend. But I really like being with you, Jimmy. It's much easier to talk to you than it was to Martin." Jimmy bows in acknowledgement of the compliment. "Maybe one day we can take another walk? Gran never goes anywhere that's fun. Once Martin drove me somewhere and we climbed a mountain. I really enjoyed that."

"Sure, we could do something like that," says Jimmy, who

has never had any inclination to scale BC's multitudinous mountains.

"And you're not angry at me?"

"What reason would I have for being angry?"

"I don't know. Martin . . ." There Janet stops, looks past Jimmy as though seeing something off in the distance, then gets into the car. Jimmy closes the door.

When they get to Janet's house, she formally thanks him. "And please thank your mother for a pleasant visit, Jimmy, and do remind Lucille to call me." She mounts the wide steps and halts a moment at the door—which has already been opened by the man servant—to ask Jimmy when she will next hear from him.

"Within a few days, I hope," Jimmy replies, put out by Janet's switch to the role of grand dame imperiously issuing orders. He waits until the wide door closes, then gets into the car and follows the circle of shrubs onto the road. Some situations, he thinks, ought never be allowed to arise, because their potential for placing an individual in a position where he might make a fool of himself is simply too great—and Jimmy is well aware he is on the verge of making a fool of himself over Janet MacDougail. He wonders if she is sitting in her bedroom at this very moment, laughing at him. Surely she must know that every man who looks at her speculates about the luscious body she keeps well hidden beneath her expensive clothes.

Still, something about Janet MacDougail's behaviour puzzles him. What is it? Ever analytic, Jimmy speculates that after meeting people Janet slips into roles that she thinks are the most fitting ones for particular occasions and individuals. That would explain why her behaviour with him fluctuates between icy haughtiness and childish, confiding intimacy. But what about her tears earlier in the evening? They seemed to flow spontaneously, didn't they? And if calculated, the effort to produce them would surely require the skills of a proficient actress and Jimmy cannot imagine how Janet could have acquired these. He recalls the unqualified expression of surprise on Janet's face when he told her about Annette's desire to find him a wife and he censures himself for attempting to pigeon-hole her. He reminds himself that if Janet were a really manipulative person, she would have proceeded with greater caution than she showed when she slipped her arm through his and said she trusted him. So, although uneasiness about Janet's behaviour lingers and he continues to fret over falling in love with a girl ten years younger than himself, he nevertheless concludes that on the whole the evening has been a success. He is sure Janet will remember his declaration of love and after a suitable period of reflection will come to accept it. It is even possible, he thinks, that one day Janet may return his love. Remembering the curve of her firm breast pressed briefly against his arm, Jimmy's doubts are lifted and he vents his high spirits by humming Handel's "See, the Conquering Hero Comes" during the remainder of the drive back to the Sung household on Union Street.

4

As a former studyholic Jimmy knows that although it is Sunday, a number of students will be hanging around the libraries and reading rooms at the university. He parks the Corolla and walks to the building that houses the commerce department. There he leans against a convenient wall, eyeing people who straggle in and out. Finally Jimmy intercepts a book-toting young man on his way out and puts his question.

"MacDougail?" the student repeats, pursing his lips. "Seems familiar, but that's about it. Sorry, I can't help you. "

Jimmy asks a few more students without having any luck, and so he decides to leave his position beside the door and penetrate the interior of the building. He locates a small room where several people sit at a table, reading and taking notes. He approaches one of the men, who shakes his head when the question is posed and vaguely waves a hand in the direction of a young woman sitting on the other side of the room.

She looks older than the average student, but wears the typical uniform—jeans, nondescript windbreaker, and tee shirt with faded words printed across the front of it. Jimmy makes one of his rapid-fire character assessments as he approaches. Some fool in the casting department sent the wrong woman out to play student. The clothes are right but the way she wears them isn't. They are much too tight and one has the impression she would like to discard them along with the role in which she has been cast. She has a hard, jaded expression and when Jimmy coughs to get her attention she says, "What do you want?"

She ignores the business card he holds out. "I've already told the police everything I know. Ask them." She gets to her feet, turns her back to Jimmy and pushes her books into a voluminous shoulder bag. Jimmy, ever observant, notes that her breasts sway with her movements and that the rear seam of her jeans is separating.

"But you did know Martin?" he persists.

"Casually." She hooks her bag over her shoulder.

"One minute. Please," Jimmy pleads.

"Fuck off." She is already hurrying from the room and ignores Jimmy as he follows.

"What's your name?" Jimmy asks, as they reach the entrance.

"Fuck off," she answers.

Only momentarily dismayed, Jimmy continues to hang around the commerce department, querying various people who pass in and out of the building. (If nothing else, Jimmy gained one important insight during his law school years. It is this: if people are willing to dig long enough, eventually they will find what they are looking for. Lawyers have learned this lesson, which is why they defend human behaviour that, on the surface, appears indefensible—they know there has to be a reason for every crime ever committed; therefore, a defence can always be found, however difficult or lengthy the search may be. What is more, lawyers know if they delve far enough, they can, so to speak, liquefy the offence and feed it back into the roots of society, thereby convincing others that the fruit which grows on the tree of perversity and violence originates, not with the accused, but with those who sit in judgment.)

Eventually he finds someone who knew Martin MacDougail. A real preppy sort of guy in top-siders, chinos and button-down shirt. The man wags his head and says, "He was kind of weird but I can't think of a reason he'd want to kill himself."

"How, weird?" Jimmy asks.

"Weird like one time our class went downtown to check out this trust company and the guy showing us around took us up onto the roof. I guess he thought we'd like to gaze out onto our future. Anyway, as soon as we get up there, Martin hops up onto the wall and starts walking around the edge. Jesus, it made me dizzy, he's like doing this high-wire act twenty-three storeys above Howe Street. The prof and the guy shepherding us around were pretty pissed off . . . you could tell Martin was not in *their* corporate future. Not that Martin gave a damn—he wasn't short of dough. But here's an idea—Martin might have been showing off, you know, doing his act on the Lions Gate Bridge, and just slipped."

Jimmy nods. "I suppose it could have happened that way. You know if Martin partied much?"

"Hell, we all party hard, I mean it's commerce, eh? Not comparative literature."

"Did he have any particular girlfriend?"

The man rubs his chin and thinks this over. "You know how it is. You see a couple together, and they're all over each other . . . you think they're in love for life. The next time you see 'em, they're doing the exact same thing, only with somebody else."

"A kind of revolving feast, eh?" Jimmy suggests.

The man grins. "Hey, great metaphor! A revolving feast . . . where a guy can sample all shapes and sizes coming around on giant trays. Sounds good to me. A dim sum, that's even better, eh?"

"Yeah, a dim sum. You know if Martin MacDougail liked to sample different women?"

"You bet he did. He took whatever came his way. Wouldn't you?"

Jimmy smirks noncommittally and asks the man whether he had seen Martin the night before his death.

"Yeah, I did. We were at the same party for a while. Then I moved on. You know how it is." Jimmy listens and nods, while thinking that individuals who know "how it is" possess a set of common understandings that allows them to converse in incomplete sentences and formulaic expressions. This particular future trust fund manager is obviously someone who knows "how it is" and no doubt always will know.

"Did you speak to Martin that evening?"

"Can't say I did. I mean . . . people came and went." He re-examines Jimmy's card. "You at law school here?" Jimmy nods. "Own business, eh? Lucrative, I suppose." He starts for the door, and Jimmy asks if he knows which woman Martin was seeing just before he died. The man rubs his square chin with its fashionable two days' growth and says, "I think I saw her around today."

"Would she happen to have short blonde hair?"

"Uh huh. And she's got lots of other stuff too . . . know what I mean?"

"Yes, but I don't know her name. Do you?"

He goes through his chin-rubbing act again. "Let's see. Barbara . . . Belinda . . . no. Betty. That's it. Betty something. Never heard a last name or if I did I didn't catch it. I would have been too busy staring."

"She's in commerce?"

"You bet. She'll probably end up in real estate, using her tits to peddle houses. Listen, I gotta run."

"One more thing. Were drugs available at the party?"

Before Jimmy finishes with his question, the door to the man's memory is slammed shut. "I wouldn't know. And anyway I never touch the stuff. Not even a couple of lines to wind down from a long week of studying. Know what I mean?" He eyes Jimmy, as though he can detect the smell of shit wafting from him, and hurries away.

Jimmy is delighted with the progress he has made in the last hour and decides to look around the main library before getting a bowl of soup at the student cafeteria. Strolling along the concourse, he recalls that when he attended UBC commerce students were described as crass, engineering students as gross, and those in education dumb; now, after being away from the university environment for a few years, Jimmy thinks maybe he understands why students in one faculty view their peers in another with such disdain: contempt is a tool of survival—a raft that helps support their shaky self-esteem and harried self-confidence as they are swept along, cascading from one academic challenge to another. He smiles as he pictures himself then, trotting around the campus with his unvarying load of books like a skinny, overworked pack animal, to and from points A, B, C and D, repeating the entire process day after dismal day.

While circulating through the library, Jimmy spots the blonde at a study carrel and goes over. "Is your name Betty?" he asks. She jumps as though a wasp has crawled beneath her and is jabbing its stinger into her bottom. Jimmy notes how her breasts vibrate.

"Who gave you the right to follow me around?" she hisses. "Clear off, or I'll complain at the front desk."

"Look, I'm not following you around," Jimmy explains. "I just want to find out if your name is Betty."

"My name is none of your business."

"The only interest I have is if you're the Betty that used to be a girlfriend of Martin MacDougail."

"That's a lie." She closes her book and prepares to leave.

"Just tell me if your name is Betty or not. Then I'll leave."

She stands by the chair, weakening defiance in every line on her face. "All right. I'm Betty Nelson. What do you want to know?"

"Anything you can tell me about Martin."

"I've already told the police everything I know."

"I understand that. But I'd appreciate if you'd go through it one more time . . . especially what you know about the Saturday night before his death."

"We had a date that evening . . . we were going out to eat before going on to a party. But Martin never showed up. So I made myself a lousy bowl of soup and went to the party on my own. That's it. End of story."

"But Martin came to the party later, didn't he?"

"Yes. And that's when I told him off. I left right after that."

"Did he explain why he'd stood you up?"

"Some tale about having to meet a cousin of his. It was his

usual bullshit. Though I suppose the guy with him could've been his cousin."

"Martin came to the party with some guy? A young guy?"

"Yeah, some kid. Maybe he wasn't even with Martin . . . I don't know . . . except they were all buddy-buddy."

"Martin didn't say if this guy was his cousin? He didn't introduce him?"

"No."

"What did he look like?"

Betty Nelson suddenly becomes uneasy. "He looked like any other young kid. Tall, fresh-faced, probably a high school kid. Anyway, I didn't care. I just wanted to leave and never set eyes on Martin again." She moves away from Jimmy, as if to escape the anger of the memory.

Jimmy gestures with spread hands, as if to erect a barrier to prevent her leaving. "I realize this is an imposition, but I'd be grateful if you'd answer a couple more questions. I'm doing this because somebody believes Martin didn't commit suicide. I've been asked to find out what really happened."

"Who asked you?"

"I'm sorry, I can't tell you that. Look, how old would you say the guy was?"

"Like I said, probably a high school kid. Under twenty, anyway . . . he'd have to be or else Martin wouldn't have him around."

Jimmy pauses before posing his next question. "You mean Martin was gay?"

"No. I mean he disliked being around people older than him. He could impress kids because he had a BMW and plenty of money to spend on them. I'm a few years older than Martin, and he couldn't hack it that I knew a little bit more than he did."

"You lived with Martin?"

"What Martin and I did is none of your business."

"I'm sorry, but I'm trying to form a picture of the kind of guy Martin was, and if you lived with him . . . well . . . you'd know him pretty well."

She hesitates before responding. "I did . . . for a little while. But he was an impossible guy to live with."

"Why?"

"You could never rely on him. You never knew what he would say or do."

"Still, you continued seeing him?"

"Only occasionally. He'd telephone, or we'd meet accidentally and he'd invite me to go somewhere with him." Betty picks up her bag and Jimmy knows his time is running out.

"Isn't there something you can add to what you've already told me?"

She hesitates and chews her lips. "Well . . . there is something, though it's probably not important . . . and I'm not sure if it was Martin I saw."

"Saw? Where?" Jimmy leans forward eagerly, waiting for her to answer.

"After I left the party that night I visited a friend—I didn't want to just go home and sit around. Anyway, later, when I was driving home from my friend's place, I thought I saw Martin walking down Broadway with someone. Perhaps I was mistaken . . . you know how it is driving at night."

"What time would that have been?"

"After midnight. You know what caught my eye? The way Martin walked. He had a real impatient walk anyway . . . only more so that night."

"And somebody was with him?"

"I could see another person walking beside him, but I don't know who."

"Could it have been the kid from the party?"

"Could have been. But I can't be sure."

"Just where on Broadway did you see him?"

"Not too far from Cambie."

"One other question. Did Martin ever use drugs?"

"I've no idea." She swings the bag onto her shoulder, and her breasts swing back.

"Surely you'd know, if you lived with him?" Jimmy says, thinking Betty Nelson must be around thirty. Still young, but some inner discontent has already cut the first lines around her lips.

"He may have experimented," she says.

"Often people go further than experimentation."

"Christ, man. What planet do you come from?" Now Betty suddenly drops the bag, sits and reopens the book she was studying when Jimmy first approached her. "I don't care what other people do," she says bitterly. "All I care about is getting my degree and making loads of money. Now, why don't you bugger off and leave me alone."

"I'll do that," Jimmy assures her. "Did Martin tell you his cousin's name?"

"I've told you, no, no, no."

"Just one more question."

"I've got a question for you."

"What is it?"

"Is it true what they say about Chinese guys?"

"What do you mean?"

Betty glances from Jimmy's eyes to his crotch and back. And as he stares uncomprehendingly, Betty raises her right hand, holds the thumb and forefinger about three centimetres apart. "You know."

A rush of anger, sadness and humiliation renders Jimmy paralyzed for a long moment. Finally he masters his feelings but cannot control a blush. Holding his head high, Jimmy Sung leaves. On the way back to his office, he thinks of sophisticated retorts like, "Surely, Ms. Nelson, you've had enough men of every race, creed and colour to know the answer to that."

He is behind his desk, still thinking, when Lucille strolls in, carrying a package of wine gums and chewing one of them. She sits on the corner of Jimmy's desk, and while removing from the package the flavours she does not like and handing them to Jimmy for disposal, she tells him they are going out to dinner at Harry Lee's cafe, after which Jimmy will accompany her to the French film now showing at the theatre on Commercial Drive. Following delivery of these marching orders, Lucille gets down to the real purpose of her visit, which is to find out more about Janet MacDougail's house. Jimmy tells Lucille it swarms with cockroaches and fleas, and that the only toilet in the place is permanently blocked, information that Lucille translates to mean Janet resides in a mansion.

Recently Lucille has taken to teasing Jimmy about having a secret cache of girlie magazines in his filing cabinet, and just before leaving the office, she maliciously taunts him not to spend the whole afternoon looking at them.

Now, it just so happens that Jimmy does have such a magazine in his file cabinet, although he has never felt uncomfortable about looking at it. Why should he? After all, Jimmy is a normal young man, and surely there's nothing wrong with the occasional peek at an air-brushed pubic zone. Today, however, is different. Jimmy experiences a sensation of guilt when Lucille reminds him of his girlie magazine; he knows why—it is due to his newly born love for Janet MacDougail, who might think less of him if she knew of its existence. Jimmy then speculates on the possibility that his feelings for Janet might affect his potency with Evelyn Chan. He recalls once reading a novel in which a man, after being contentedly married for a number of years, falls madly in love with another woman and finds he cannot make love with his wife. Jimmy unlocks the file cabinet, takes out the magazine, looks at a few pictures and is reassured when he experiences some stirrings. He returns the magazine to the file cabinet and goes down to the store, where he bags up the day's takings and carries them to the bank. From there he goes to Harry Lee's, where Annette and Lucille are busily informing Harry that Jimmy is as good as married to a wealthy Caucasian woman.

Harry Lee purchases fruits and vegetables for his restaurant from Annette and is one of her greatest admirers. For many years Harry remained unmarried, and Jimmy never understood why Harry had not proposed marriage to Annette, until it gradually dawned on him that maybe Harry *had* proposed but she had turned him down. Now he is married to a tiny, bad-tempered woman who ferociously bullies him. She has borne one female child, who shows promise of being as big a bully as her mother.

"Just wait until you see her," Annette is saying to Harry, as Jimmy joins them at a table. "A tall Caucasian goddess." For a moment Jimmy feels like giving Annette a hard poke in the ribs, but of course he would never actually do such a thing.

"Ignore everything Mother says," Jimmy tells Harry.

Harry promptly rejects the suggestion and says, "I can't believe Jimmy's finally got himself a girl. Mind you," he quickly adds, "I always knew he'd eventually find one. It was just a matter of time. Look at me. It took me years." At that moment, his wife Emily appears at the table and directs Harry back to the pans in the kitchen.

"What you going to order?" Emily ungraciously asks. Annette, oblivious as always to Emily's disapproval of her relationship with Harry, proceeds to order dinner, instructing Emily on how Harry should prepare each dish.

"I'll never understand why Harry married that battle-axe," Annette says after Emily has left.

"Look, Mother," Jimmy says, "I wish you would stop talking about Janet MacDougail."

"Janet thinks a lot of you, Jimmy," Annette says. "Doesn't she, Lucille?"

"That's what she told me," Lucille tells Jimmy as she pats his hand. "She says you're easy to talk to."

"So's a stuffed teddy bear," Jimmy snaps. "I've warned her about you two. The last thing Janet is thinking about is getting married. She doesn't even have a boyfriend, and what's more she doesn't want one."

Annette picks up her chopsticks and waves them triumphantly. "That's exactly what I said when I was Janet's age, and six months later I was married to your father. Don't get the idea that Janet's family is any better than ours. Uncle Jimmy says the MacDougails are a pretty shady lot."

"And what exactly does that mean?" Jimmy demands.

Annette shrugs her shoulders, while Lucille watches and

giggles. She enjoys it when Annette works Jimmy over. "Ask him yourself."

"I did," replies Jimmy, "and Uncle Jimmy told me he knows the family only casually. Those were his exact words. Listen, Mother, if Uncle Jimmy's told you something he hasn't told me, I want to know what it is."

"You're the detective," Annette says. "Anyway, it's no big deal."

Jimmy, knowing it is useless to try to get anything more out of Annette, drops the subject and concentrates on eating. After the meal, which Annette pays for, Jimmy and Lucille drive Annette home and then go on to the cinema, where they try to follow the dialogue by reading the blurred sub-titles. For most of the film, Lucille lies with her head on Jimmy's shoulder, apparently asleep. She perks up during the bedroom scenes, whereas Jimmy finds them boring because the more interesting parts of the actors' bodies are not shown. How easy it is to deceive people, he thinks. For instance, from the rear, he and Lucille might be taken for lovers, whereas the truth is, Lucille is using him as a convenient pillow. The film ends and they go to a nearby restaurant where they eat coconut cream pie and drink coca-cola. Lucille tries to bring up the subject of Janet MacDougail, but Jimmy resolutely sticks to criticizing the film.

"It was a hodgepodge," Jimmy pontificates. "Couldn't make up its mind whether to be a commercial Hollywood movie or a European art film."

"I knew you and Janet would take to each other the minute I saw her," Lucille says.

"You don't know anything," Jimmy snarls. "So for a change, why not concentrate on running your own life, instead of interfering in mine."

"My life goes along perfectly well, but yours is one big screw-up." How can Jimmy defend himself against this withering accusation? He knows better than Lucille that his life has been ridiculous at best since the day he ceased being a whiz kid. Her remark only serves to intensify the uncertainties experienced by him earlier in the day, and these are revived the next morning when he methodically ascends the twenty stairs to his office. He moons around, spending a lot of time at the window, glumly watching people in the street below. *They,* he thinks, know how to manage their lives—why can't he? Finally, after leaving another message at police headquarters, Jimmy leaves the office and walks to Harry Lee's for a cup of coffee. There he has the misfortune of running into Uncle Jimmy and Sam Mackintosh.

"Nephew," his uncle calls as he spots Jimmy entering the cafe. "Taking another coffee break?" It is almost noon, but Jimmy supposes noontime is early for people like Uncle Jimmy and Sam who go to bed closer to sunrise than midnight. He sits with the older men.

"How do you think Nephew is looking these days, Sam?" Uncle Jimmy says.

"Pretty good I'd say," Sam replies.

"You know, Sam, sometimes I wish I'd taken up the law. There's no doubt it puts a nice finishing touch on a man. You agree, Sam?" says Uncle Jimmy.

"You betcha!" says Sam.

"Mother says you know something about the MacDougail family, Uncle," Jimmy now says.

"I do," agrees his uncle. "They're a family who vigorously practise what they preach, which is—what you think is rightfully yours is actually theirs. In other words, they're much like everyone else in the world."

"Know something, James?" Sam says. "One time a guy told me Mac pushed a few pills, maybe some reefer, even some skag or snow."

"Wait a bit, wait a bit, Sam," Jimmy says. "Are you saying you know someone named Mac who sells drugs?"

"That's what I heard. Mind you, Mac don't come by much. He just shows up every so often and hands a bottle around."

"And you've heard he's involved in drug trafficking?"

Sam shrugs, as Uncle Jimmy speaks for him. "Sam's merely passing on a rumour, Nephew."

"Have you seen this man lately, Sam?"

"Can't say as I have."

"But you know him to speak to?"

"Sure, we've been juicers together a time or two."

"Would you introduce me to him?"

"Dunno about that," Sam says, looking uneasy.

"I think it's a bad idea," Uncle Jimmy remarks. "I doubt if the MacDougails would want you to be contacting one of their family rejects."

"Oh, you doubt it, do you?" Jimmy's banked anger flares up. "Forget it!" He jumps up and hurries from the cafe, unable to put up with what he perceives as insulting treatment by his uncle. He strides along Main Street to police headquarters, only to be told Sergeant Robson is not expected back until later in the afternoon. Jimmy leaves yet another message and decides to wheel his beater up to the Pacific Press building to check out the news reports of Martin MacDougail's death. But he learns nothing new there. Disgruntled and depressed, he goes back to his office, asking himself how he can legitimately continue the farce of his investigation. As he opens the door, the phone rings.

"Have you discovered anything new?" Janet asks, without bothering to identify herself.

"A little," Jimmy replies, and goes on to narrate his discussion with Betty Nelson. "I'll probably talk to her again. I dare say she remembers more than she realizes. And I had the feeling she was holding something back. After all, she lived with Martin and must know something about his life. Didn't he ever mention her?"

"No." The voice is very remote, as if Janet has retreated from the phone. "Martin lived by himself."

"But there's no reason for Betty Nelson to lie, is there?" He waits, expecting Janet to signify agreement. When she does not respond, he continues, "You're sure Martin never mentioned her name?"

"Never." Janet's voice is now even fainter.

Jimmy persists. "But he must have spoken to you about his girlfriends. Remember? You gave me a list."

"Yes. But I don't remember a Betty."

"Okay. I'll keep asking around. One other point. Do you know if a cousin of yours was in town the weekend Martin died?"

"I . . ." She hesitates, then replies, "I don't know. Gran doesn't tell me everything."

"I see," Jimmy gently says. "Isn't it possible Martin didn't tell you everything either?"

"He told me most things."

Jimmy does not contradict Janet, but wonders if people ever do tell the truth about their private lives. He, personally, does not. "Betty Nelson did tell me something that may turn out to be important. After she left the party that night, she went over to a friend's place and didn't leave there until after midnight. On her way home she's pretty sure she saw Martin walking along Broadway with someone—maybe the same guy she'd seen at the party. And don't forget, it was at Broadway and Main you saw Martin talking to some girl."

"Oh! You've found out a lot already."

Jimmy experiences a surge of pleasure, hearing Janet's compliment. "It depends how you look at it," he says. "I haven't been able to contact the officer in charge of the police investigation yet, so I've no idea what he's uncovered. I'll go back to UBC tomorrow and try to locate more people who knew your brother. But I also want you to try and remember if Martin mentioned someone named Betty."

"I'm not much good at remembering details."

"Please try," Jimmy urges. "And I should tell you, once I've done these things, I doubt if there's much more I can do."

"You have to do more." Janet's voice strengthens. "You promised you'd find out what really happened."

"No, Janet. I only said I'd make sure the police investigation had been thorough."

"You promised."

"No, I didn't, Janet."

"You did! " she haughtily replies and bangs down the telephone. Jimmy kicks the long-suffering desk leg, and after replacing the receiver, stares at the desk top and wishes Janet MacDougail had never found his name in the Yellow Pages.

When the phone rings again, Jimmy snatches it up and hears Janet say, "I'm sorry. I shouldn't have hung up."

Jimmy forcefully replies, "I intend to do everything I can to help you, Janet, but there's a limit to what I'm able to do. I'm not Superman."

"Well then, I guess I'll just have to make the best of it, won't I?" She replaces the phone before Jimmy has a chance to reply.

At the dinner table that evening Annette announces that Uncle Jimmy is planning to spend the entire summer in Vancouver. Jimmy groans, and is about to say he hopes his uncle will stay clear of him, when Lucille pipes up to inform him that Janet thinks he is making progress in his investigation of her brother's death.

"How do you know what Janet thinks?" Jimmy demands.

"She phoned me just before you came home." Lucille looks so smug Jimmy would like to dunk her into a pool of icy water; afterwards, when his mother and Lucille commence a lengthy discussion about the clothes Lucille is going to take to Janet's for the weekend, Jimmy is barely able to restrain himself from telling Lucille not to forget to pack her mink coat and diamond tiara. In any case, they ignore him, while Annette suggests Lucille call in at Mrs. Liu's if she needs anything. Annette makes no bones about it—she will not allow any daughter of hers to enter the home of a wealthy person wearing clothes that are not up to sartorial scratch. Jimmy retires from the foray, defeated. He watches a TV program for a while and then goes to bed. He dreams he is walking with Janet in a garden where masses of beautiful flowers shimmer like sun-flecked rippling water. Janet moves ahead of him, and as Jimmy tries to overtake her, she commences to remove her clothes. This arouses conflict in Jimmy. On the one hand, he longs to see Janet naked; on the other, he does not want her body to be revealed to the people who have appeared in the garden. His heart thumps as he watches Janet slip off her skirt and blouse, which are immediately replaced by others. The dream ends as Janet walks into the centre of a huge cluster of flowers, which seem to rise up and embrace her. She turns to look back at Jimmy, and he sees she now has the face of Lucille and the body of Evelyn Chan. As the dream fades, Jimmy awakes to the jangle of his alarm. It is five-thirty, time to get up and take Annette to the wholesale produce market.

As always, Annette is already up, waiting for Jimmy with a cup of coffee. But before going down the steep, narrow stairs into the kitchen, Jimmy carefully opens the door to Lucille's room and listens to her quiet breathing. He knows he has no real reason to worry, but he is always slightly uneasy about leaving Lucille sleeping alone in the house.

In the half-light of dawn, Jimmy drives Annette to the busy market where she examines produce samples while he buys two styrofoam cups of coffee and trails around after her, enjoying the sights and scents. Jimmy marvels that his mother has been following this same daily routine for as long as he can remember, always purchasing the same ratio of produce, three-quarters Chinese, one-quarter western. One head of iceberg lettuce to every three of bok choy. As far as he knows, she has never been ill a single day or taken a holiday. Jimmy is in awe of his mother; he believes she is filled with a strength of body and character far beyond what most people possess. (Jimmy recalls that Herman Melville, author of *Moby Dick*, wrote that what seemed to exceptional and heroic to land-bound people was nothing more than daily routine for whalers. Jimmy places Annette among that select group of people who, like the whalers, perform astonishing feats each day without realizing they do so, never looking back on what they have done, but always ahead to what still needs doing.)

Because of the way Jimmy feels about his mother, he appears less worthy to himself than he really is; later in the morning while he sits in his office, reviewing the newspaper articles he has photocopied at the *Sun* office, he begins seriously to doubt his ability to produce a satisfactory explanation for Martin MacDougail's death. He wonders if Betty Nelson ever told the police about seeing Martin walking along Broadway that night, and considers the possibility the police may already know and regard it as unimportant. Of course, Jimmy can never know what the police think unless they tell him, and that seems more and more unlikely. Jimmy decides to telephone the police station again and is not surprised when he is informed Sergeant Robson is unavailable for his call.

Jimmy decides it is imperative to interview Betty Nelson again. Urgency grips him, and he gallops down the stairs, tells Annette he is going out to UBC, puts some apples and a couple of bananas into a bag, gets into Annette's Corolla and takes off.

But the hectic rushing around does not do him any good. Jimmy hangs around the entrance to the commerce building for a while before seeing anyone. Finally, the student he spoke to on Sunday shows up—the future manager of old money— and Jimmy asks if he has seen Betty Nelson around.

"Nope. But if I do, I'll tell her you're looking for her." He winks, a male conspiratorial wink.

Jimmy is not too happy about Betty Nelson knowing he is looking for her, but realizes the young man's offer is better than nothing. "Thanks. Tell her I'll wait in the cafeteria near the library."

Jimmy spends another fifteen minutes asking around, but doesn't get anywhere. Finally he goes to the cafeteria, where he buys a bran muffin and a cup of coffee and sits at a small table by himself. As he is about to bite into one of his apples, a young woman appears beside the table and asks if she can sit there.

The woman's small, compact body inclines toward the left, due to the heavy pack sack dragging on her shoulder, which thuds as she drops it to the floor. Her round, pleasant, alabaster face is partly hidden by a pair of heavy-framed glasses, behind which her exceptionally large, brown eyes examine Jimmy with eager curiosity. Her black hair is pulled back and held in place at the nape of her neck with a piece of yellow wool.

"Phew!" she says, as she places a mug of hot chocolate and an egg salad sandwich on the table. "By the time I get through university I'll have a permanent list to my body."

"Why not wear two packs?" suggests Jimmy.

She laughs and unwraps her sandwich. "That's what I should be eating more of," she says, pointing to Jimmy's apple, "but I never seem to get anywhere near a store." Jimmy reaches into his bag, brings out a red-faced Spartan, and offers it to her. "Oh no. Really . . ."

"My mother owns a produce store."

"Lucky you." She takes a bite and places the apple beside the sandwich. "There! A balanced meal. My first in months. So, what're you taking this semester?"

"Nothing. I'm not a student. I'm here for other reasons."

"Teaching?" she quizzes.

Jimmy smiles and shakes his head. He thinks he knows which faculty she is enrolled in, but asks anyway.

"Education—primary grades." She laughs. "If I didn't have to haul this clutter around, I'd be having a ball."

"Honestly?" Jimmy finds it hard to believe anyone can enjoy attending university.

"You bet! I love it here! Guess where I'm from." Jimmy shakes his head, refusing to speculate. "Atlin!" she announces. When she gets no reaction she goes on, "It's north of Prince Rupert, you've heard of Rupert? Well, you just keep going on past Rupert and pray you don't miss Atlin." She picks up the apple and eyes it hungrily. "You know, every time I walk into the libraries here I get high, you know, kinda tipsy, just thinking about all those books on the shelves, waiting there for me to read. I can hardly believe my good fortune." She takes another bite of the apple and juice oozes from between her lips. "Ooh, that's delicious. You know what I'm thinking? I'm thinking you're thinking here's another one of those Jews who're fascinated by learning—and you'd be right on both counts: I am Jewish and I do think learning is the most wonderful thing in the world."

"Your people and mine share the same stereotype." Jimmy takes out one of his business cards and hands it to her. She examines it, front and back, while Jimmy says, "I was sixteen when I came to UBC and people called me a whiz kid. Now, when I look back, I see I was more like a dumb rat trying to gnaw its way through a huge, endless wall."

"What can I say? So now you're a successful lawyer?"

"Hardly," Jimmy counters. "I whizzed through university, whizzed on to law school, then whizzed into a judge's law library where my whiz suddenly vanished."

She nibbles at the apple core. "You probably needed a rest. After I get my B.Ed. I'm going to work just long enough to save enough money to come back for my M.Ed. Then I'll work for a while longer, and come back for my doctorate."

"And then?"

"I haven't made up my mind, but I'm pretty sure I'll want to go on learning. It's the only thing I really like doing."

Jimmy offers her another apple. "Take it," Jimmy says. "Anybody who's prepared to do all that learning deserves an extra apple."

She laughs and accepts the apple, then asks what Jimmy is doing on campus. Jimmy provides an abbreviated explanation.

"You know something," she tells him when he has run out of steam. "I think I may have met that guy you're talking about."

"It would be an amazing coincidence if you had," Jimmy says, upset with himself for failing to have a photograph of Martin MacDougail to show around.

The girl then tells Jimmy she and her roommate were sitting one day in the cafeteria in the Faculty of Education building when a man they didn't know approached their table. "He told us he was meeting a friend, who hadn't showed up yet. He asked if he could sit down and chat with us while he waited. The guy told us he was taking mostly commerce courses, but knew quite a few education students—like the friend he was meeting—and really liked them. He started talking about this party he was throwing on the weekend and asked if we wanted to come. But we never went because my roommate came down with the flu, and I didn't want to go alone, especially not all the way across Vancouver in her car."

"I doubt if it was the same guy. MacDougail lived in Point Grey."

"Well, this place was someplace on the east side. My friend and I checked it out on a city map. I wrote the address he gave us in one of my notebooks. Would you like it?" She leans over to upend her pack, tumbling textbooks, ring binders and assorted notebooks onto the floor. "Now which one was it?" She stares at the jumble of books and finally selects one and thumbs through it until she finds a page covered with notes and diagrams. "There!" she triumphantly says and points to a scribble in the corner of the page.

"Can I see it?" Jimmy asks. She hands over the notebook and he sees that the street, just as she said, is located in East Vancouver in the Commercial Drive area, close to the harbour.

Jimmy writes down the address, then returns her notebook. "Maybe you should give me your name and a phone number where I can reach you."

"Sure. It's Rebecca," she tells him. "Rebecca Golden. Totally, unmistakenly Jewish."

"Would you prefer to be something else?" he asks.

"Oh no. I like being Jewish and having thousands of years of history behind me.

"I feel much the same way about being Chinese," Jimmy tells her.

"You're lucky there's a Chinatown here. You know, it's funny, but a lot of people think it's odd for a Golden to come from Atlin. But I tell them there's Goldens in them thar hills." They both laugh. Rebecca crams everything back into her pack and stands, hoisting the pack onto her left shoulder. "You think I'll make out all right, you know, trying to get my three degrees?"

"I think you'll end crammed with wisdom," he says.

"Thanks." She laughs. "I suppose you got firsts all the time."

"I'm afraid so," Jimmy admits.

She sighs as they walk together out of the cafeteria. "Lucky you. I get mostly seconds." They stop by the entrance.

"I'd sure like to know if that guy who killed himself was the same one who invited us to his party."

"I'll do my best to let you know," Jimmy promises.

"And thanks for the apples." Rebecca smiles and hurries off, her left shoulder sagging.

Most of the paint is eroded off the cedar siding of the East End house and Jimmy, sitting in the Corolla across the street, finds it hard to believe anyone has lived in it in recent years. He thinks maybe (probably) he is on a wild goose chase but decides to find out if the house is occupied before going back to the office. He knocks, then bangs on the door. When there is no answer, he tries the knob and is surprised when it turns and the door opens. Jimmy does not make a habit of entering houses uninvited, but decides in this instance he is justified.

The room Jimmy enters is filled with that peculiar scent that emanates from old furniture. He sees a plastic-topped table, two chrome kitchen chairs, a love seat edging toward disintegration, and something that looks as much out of place as a giraffe at a gathering of crocodiles—a new, uncovered studio bed. From there, Jimmy goes into a small kitchen, which holds a stained sink, a filthy gas stove and an ancient refrigerator. Off the kitchen is a tiny bathroom, barely containing a waterless lavatory pan and a tin-walled shower stall. Near the refrigerator is a locked door that, after a moment of indecision, Jimmy kicks open in the decisive manner he has witnessed on TV cop shows. Beyond the door is a flight of carpet-covered stairs.

He cautiously ascends the stairs and enters a small, windowless room; at first he is preoccupied with the furniture and does not notice that light is flooding in through skylights set into the ceiling. Everything in the room is white—wall-to-wall carpeting, brocaded wallpaper, leather armchairs and the pedestal that supports a glass coffee table top. On one wall hangs a white-framed reproduction of Picasso clowns; on another, an enlarged, white-framed black-and-white photograph of a naked child, a girl about ten years old. She seems to stare directly at Jimmy, and he blinks to dispel the feeling she is physically present in the room. Her lips are tentatively parted, the childish down on her forearms and mons veneris is highlighted. She presents a perfect image of prepubescent expectancy.

Jimmy leaves the room, glances into a white, aseptically immaculate bathroom, then passes into another white room in which most of the space is taken by a large brass bed. On a white-legged table beside the bed sits a jarring intrusion into the carefully arranged decor—a paper cup. But none of this matters to Jimmy, who is now staring at a woman lying face down on the bed. His first reaction is to back out and scurry down the stairs and out of the house, thinking the woman is asleep; but gradually it dawns on Jimmy she might be dead. He kneels down to get a closer look and is horrified when he sees it is Betty Nelson and she definitely is not alive.

Jimmy has read enough detective stories to know that private investigators are invariably detached and controlled when they find a dead body; what is more, for reasons never fully clarified in these stories, they are slow to inform the police of morbid discoveries. Usually they prefer to stand over the body making hardbitten wisecracks. But Jimmy has nothing to say as he stares at the body of Betty Nelson.

He turns away and runs from the house so quickly he cannot remember having done so, races to the nearest gas station and telephones the police.

Now back at the house, Jimmy waits outside on the sidewalk until he sees several uniformed and plain-clothed police officers emerge from an unmarked car and two patrol vehicles. He hurries forward to tell his story and is surprised when the officer in charge does not seem to doubt what he says. Later, when the officer introduces himself and Jimmy realizes he has finally made contact with Sergeant Robson, he wonders if he might never have met the man had he not discovered someone dead.

"Let's go over your story once more, Mr. Sung," Robson says, as everyone clusters around the bed. "Hm! You say you met this woman out at UBC. Right?" Jimmy volubly explains how and where he met Betty Nelson, while Robson nods and periodically releases guttural, explosive "Hm's" that make Jimmy blink nervously. "Hm! Was it Betty Nelson who told you about this house?"

Jimmy rushes on to tell Robson about his chance encounter with Rebecca Golden. "Hm! Hm!" Robson comments. "Be careful with that cup," he yells at a uniformed officer. "Bag it, and the contents too! You were saying, Mr. Sung?" But Robson does not wait for Jimmy to continue the saga; instead he speaks to the physician whom he has called to the scene. "So, what d'you think, Doctor?"

The physician, who looks no older than Jimmy, shrugs. "I'd say an overdose of some drug. She can be turned over now." Two police officers bend over to raise and turn the body, but Robson halts them mid-way, takes a handkerchief from his pants pocket and reaches into the place where the body has lain to retrieve a hypodermic needle. This he then drops into a bag held open by another officer. The doctor leans down and points to a bruise in the crook of her elbow. "That could be where the needle went in," he says.

"Hm! " Robson says. "How long you figure she's been dead?"

"Between twelve and twenty-four hours. We'll have a better idea after the autopsy."

Robson orders the body to be taken away. "Let's go into the other room," he says to Jimmy, then turns to the officer who is clearly his immediate subordinate. "Stop gawking at her, Dougherty and see if you can find her handbag. It has to be someplace. We need something to go on."

Robson is no taller than Jimmy, but the solidity of his

body leaves the impression he is twice Jimmy's size. His light brown hair is worn in a brush cut, and while his blue-grey eyes set in a ruddy-complexioned face are small, they glow with a fierce, crackling energy. He is dressed in a dark grey suit, black shoes and colour-coordinated shirt and tie. "Classy furniture, eh?" he says to Jimmy as they seat themselves in the white chairs. "Hm! Okay, now tell me again how you became involved in all this." He listens intently, nods and periodically lets out "Hm's" as Jimmy goes through the story of his first meeting with Janet MacDougail, pausing only for a second or two as the bag containing Betty Nelson's body is being carried through the room and down the stairs. Jimmy ends his tale by saying he hopes Robson has no objection to his conducting an investigation into the death of his client's brother.

Robson shrugs. "I doubt if you'll come up with anything more than we have." He waves a large hand around the room. "What do you make of all this?" He stands and goes into the bedroom, where two officers are crawling on the floor. "Found anything yet?" He turns back to Jimmy. "Let's go," he says. "And don't forget to seal the place, Dougherty," he orders before stomping down the stairs, followed by Jimmy. In the street, officers are posted near the entrance and several people stand at a distance, watching. Robson orders officers to question the neighbours and to check cars parked in the area. He looks at Jimmy and says, "Let's see what's at the back." Jimmy follows obediently, and the two men find themselves in a small yard filled with wind-deposited litter. The back steps of the house are gone and the door boarded up. "Illegal," Robson says, pointing to the door. "Fire regulations." He looks along the alley and shakes his head. "This area's sure run-down. Look at that." Robson points to a rust-corroded shell of a stripped-down car in the alley. "Where do you live, Mr. Sung?" he asks. When Jimmy supplies him with his address, he says, "Hm! Chinatown, eh?" Then adds, "You sure you've told me everything?"

"The little I know," Jimmy says. "Of course I haven't had an opportunity to see your report."

"I'd say you know as much about MacDougail's death as

I do," Robson says. "When you interviewed the deceased, how did she seem? Unhappy? Depressed?"

"She seemed angry at how MacDougail treated her."

"Wonder why we never found out she'd lived with him? Hm! Anyway, all the evidence pointed to a suicide. The Mac-Dougails didn't want any fuss made over it, and so we were happy enough to close the case." Robson walks back to the street and Jimmy dutifully follows. "So the girl doesn't think her brother killed himself, eh?"

"She claims he would never commit suicide. I don't know if it's any good as corroborative evidence, but a guy I talked to out at UBC who took some courses with him told me Martin got a big thrill out of doing dangerous things, that he liked scaring people. He said he once saw Martin climb onto the parapet of a downtown office building and walk around the edge."

"Hm! That suggests MacDougail was the type of guy who needed an audience, which means somebody could have been there on the bridge with him. Exhibitionists never perform unless somebody's around to watch, like flashers don't wave their peckers around in empty playgrounds."

"Was there an autopsy?" Jimmy asks.

"Sure. It's routine." Robson jabs a thumb at the shabby house. "You know there's something fishy about that set-up. It doesn't add up."

"Did you interview Martin's buddies?"

"Martin MacDougail may have had a lot of acquaintances, but he had no friends. Anyway, most of the people we interviewed were women. A few told us they had hopped into the sack with him, but the dead woman wasn't among them. You sure Betty Nelson said she was shacked up with MacDougail?"

"Yes, but only for a short while."

"Odd we missed that. Sloppy interviewing, maybe."

"Janet MacDougail told me her brother had promised to take her out in his new sports car on the morning he died."

"That means bugger-all. Suicides often broadcast plans they don't intend to carry out. Hm! I hate this sort of case. You don't know where to begin—yet the beginning often turns out to be the most important part. Hm! What did you make of the decor in that place, Mr. Sung?" Robson turns away to call an officer. "Hey, Jack! I'm leaving. See you later." He swings back to Jimmy. "Let's go have a cappuccino. There's a coffee bar on Commercial Drive."

"Which one?" says Jimmy.

"Follow me." Robson goes to his car while Jimmy scrambles to his. He sees Robson drive off like a teenager, one hand on the steering wheel and an arm and hand resting on the open window. Robson parks on the busy street in front of a fire hydrant, leaving Jimmy to search for a parking spot further along. Robson is already seated at a table when Jimmy enters the dark cafe, where men sit at small tables scattered around the room or stand by the small coffee bar, conversing in Italian. "I ordered two cappuccinos," Robson says, as the proprietor carries two foam-topped cups to the table. Jimmy is surprised when Robson speaks to the man in fluent Italian. "My maternal grandparents are Italian," Robson tells Jimmy. "Ma lectured me in Italian while she whacked my ass for being a bad boy."

"You know these guys?" asks Jimmy.

"Some of them. They love to talk. Italians are great for gossiping."

"Like the Chinese."

"Like everybody I guess. Well, it's easier on the back than working, and talking with people is a helluva lot better than fighting and killing 'em. Right?" As Robson talks he also scans the room, and Jimmy wonders if police officers automatically case every place they enter and categorize the people in it according to their criminal potential. Jimmy finds Robson's behaviour unsettling; it leaves him with the impression the policeman is not listening to what he is saying; yet when he checks Robson's responses, it is clear he misses nothing.

"What have you found out about the MacDougail family?" Robson asks.

"Not much."

"Did Martin's sister say she knew Betty Nelson?"

"She's positive she never heard of her. My guess is Janet actually knows very little about her brother's life. I asked her to give me a list of names of his friends and all she could do was write out a list of first names, and they're all girls."

"You have the list with you?" Jimmy takes out the piece of paper and hands it over. Robson examines it, then folds and puts it in the inside pocket of his jacket. "I'll have a copy made and return it. And maybe I'll have a chat with the sister too, even though Mrs. MacDougail is very definite that Martin hardly ever came to the house."

"According to Janet, he'd sneak in at night to see her. He'd come in through a side door and go directly up to Janet's room. Apparently the grandmother disapproved of Martin's drinking."

"That's not surprising," Robson interjects. "There's some shadowy alcoholic uncle in the background."

"Hey, wait a minute! That may be the man Sam Mackintosh was telling me about."

"So what about him?"

"He periodically shows up at Victory Square."

Robson shrugs—he's not really interested. He has to deal with Betty Nelson's death. "I guess it could be the same guy."

"Sam says the talk is he used to deal in drugs."

"That wouldn't surprise me; guys that hang around that park dabble in everything. Anyway, Mrs. MacDougail clammed up when I asked about Martin's uncle. She said she didn't know where her son was living or what he was doing. People like the MacDougails don't like the smell of failure."

"Is there much money in the family? I asked Janet about the their finances but she knew next to nothing."

"You've never heard of MacDougail, Incorporated in the US? Well, the BC MacDougails are part of that family—but don't ask me which part. Hell, I had enough trouble squeezing that little bit of information out of the old lady."

Jimmy smiles. "Not exactly helpful, is she?"

"I guess it's understandable. She's got one son boozing himself to death and another one who managed to blow himself and his wife up in a boating accident. And she's left to raise two little kids and make sure a helluva big trust fund isn't drained away by a bunch of shyster lawyers."

"You know if the grandmother has money of her own?"

"She acts as if she's got truckloads of the stuff. Are you suggesting Martin's death is related to money?"

"No. But I think something else may be related." Jimmy tells Robson about Janet seeing her brother standing on Broadway, talking to a woman who might have been a prostitute.

Robson shrugs. "Maybe MacDougail liked to pay for it."

"But he didn't need to," Jimmy protests. "He had plenty of women to go to bed with, Betty Nelson for one."

"Take it from me, Mr. Sung, there's some real nut cases out there when it comes to sex. Maybe he liked ugly women or pretty boys. Could have had a shoe fetish. I knew a guy who could only do it when Tennessee Ernie Ford records were playing. Imagine getting turned on by "Sixteen Tons"! Who knows? But right now, I'm more interested in finding out what Betty Nelson was doing in that house."

"Since she lived with Martin for a while she probably knew about the house—maybe it was a meeting place. And don't forget Rebecca Golden was invited to a party there."

"Hm! I didn't see any evidence of partying going on."

"Look, I'd like to make a suggestion."

"Go right ahead," Robson says.

"I think it's possible Martin took prostitutes to the house. And maybe . . . you know . . . maybe he got in somebody's way."

"You mean a pimp! Hell, a pimp'd just beat MacDougail up. No, that doesn't compute, Mr. Sung."

"Suppose narcotics were involved?"

"Hm! That makes more sense." Robson raises his hand for two more coffees.

"So somebody decides to get rid of Martin and make it look like a suicide. And afterwards the murderer gets the idea that Martin might have told Betty Nelson something about him. So he decides to eliminate her as well."

"Aren't you forgetting something, Mr. Sung? We don't know if Betty Nelson was murdered."

"I'm not forgetting. But why would she go to that house to kill herself? It doesn't make sense. When I was talking to her that day out at UBC she seemed angry at Martin. I'm not sure . . . but maybe what I took for anger was really fear."

The proprietor now appears at the table with two more cappuccinos. Jimmy offers to pay, but the man waves the bill away and returns to the bar. Robson laughs. "There's something to be said for being a cop, eh? But don't swallow everything you hear about cops being on the take. Actually, it's a bugger of a life." He noisily sucks in coffee. "Ever thought of joining the police force? I mean, there's an overabundance of lawyers in Vancouver, and we sure could use a few more guys who speak Chinese. Anyway, I'll bet you're not raking in that much dough."

"I manage," Jimmy murmurs.

"Hm . . ." Robson stares fixedly at Jimmy. "Let's think for a minute . . . a lot of dope comes through Vancouver . . ." Robson rocks back in his chair and continues to transfix Jimmy with his glare. "Christ! If I thought . . ." He lowers his chair with such force that Jimmy expects the chair legs to shatter and is rather disappointed when they don't. "No. It can't be that. There's not a shred of evidence pointing to drugs. Not a single thing."

"Were you looking for a drug connection?" Jimmy asks.

"No. Let's go over this again. Janet MacDougail tells you she sees her brother one night on Broadway talking to a woman who may be a prostitute. Did she say where on Broadway?"

"Broadway and Main."

"Okay. Now, let's get this story straight. The dead woman also tells you she saw MacDougail close to where his sister saw him. So would Betty Nelson have told anyone else what she saw?"

"Did she tell the police?"

"I dunno. I'll have to check the file. Goddamn it! I thought today was going to be easy for a change. I think I'll call in and get somebody to go over it." Robson stands, goes to the bar, and uses the telephone. After a few minutes he returns to the table and tells Jimmy he has decided to go to Martin's apartment to have another look around. "Want to come?" he asks, and without waiting for Jimmy's reply, walks out, calling over his shoulder, "Follow me," leaving Jimmy to run to the Corolla. By the time Robson is parking his car in front of an apartment block in Point Grey, Jimmy is enraged. He has gone through two red lights and narrowly escaped an accident, all in an effort to keep up with a law enforcement officer who exceeds the posted speed limit and weaves in and out of traffic like a crazed adolescent joy rider. Then, to cap it, after Jimmy parks the car two blocks away and hurries to join Robson in front of the apartment building, Robson barks, "Where the hell you been?"

"Parking my car," snaps Jimmy.

"Why didn't you pull up behind me? You're with me, see, so park where I do." Robson stabs the doorbell of the building manager's suite. "Sergeant Robson, Vancouver Police," he announces. "I want you to open the MacDougail apartment for me."

An elderly, overweight manager comes to the door and escorts them to the apartment. While riding up in the elevator he explains he has been managing the apartment building alone since his wife died. After he unlocks the door he turns to leave. "Wait a minute," Robson says. "Nobody's been inside this apartment since the police were here? Right?"

"Now let me see." The manager pulls his left ear, as if the gesture will trigger his memory. "Oh yes . . . now I remember. The former occupant's brother came by one day to collect some books."

"Oh yeah? When was that?" Robson quietly asks, the personification of politeness.

The manager does more ear-tugging. "Now let me see . . . it was one afternoon last week. Thursday? Yes . . . that's right . . . it was Thursday."

"Did you see the books the guy took away?"

"Nooo. They were in a small bag . . . a flight bag."

"Did you see the man put the books into the bag?"

"Nooo. I opened the door to the suite for him. Such a pleasant young man . . . so upset over his brother's death."

"Okay, I'll let you know when I'm ready to leave."

The manager smiles, gives a little bow and departs. Robson closes the apartment door and leans against it. "That fat idiot! He should of known better, he should of telephoned Mrs. MacDougail to check on that guy before he let him in. Goddamn it! Punks don't even have to commit a B and E anymore, fools like Lardass open the doors wide and invite 'em in! Kee-rist! If there were any drugs in this dump, they're sure as hell gone by now. Jesus! Why didn't I give this place a going over? Eh, can you tell me that?" Robson's eyes bulge as he pokes a finger at Jimmy's nose. "Well, I'll tell you why. Because I wanted an easy out—yeah, that's it—I wanted a suicide, that's why. And so I couldn't even be bothered to give this place a shakedown. How dumb can you be?" Suddenly Robson calms down. Self-condemnation departs and is replaced by professional objectivity. "Okay. Let's have a look-see."

While Robson goes into the bedroom, Jimmy looks through Martin MacDougail's collection of books—a sampling of paperbacks, a couple of sex manuals and a brown-paper-wrapped book filled with glossy pictures of young naked girls, which he shows to Robson.

Robson thumbs through the photos. "Sonofabitch! So the guy was probably a pedophile too! Jesus!" He goes back to pulling out and emptying drawers and overturning furniture. Jimmy, always eager to learn from an expert, observes the havoc Robson leaves behind as he moves from room to room. Finally the two men find themselves in the bedroom, standing amidst the chaos, grimly looking at a massive, wood-framed waterbed. They get down on their knees at either side of the bed to peer between the bed frame and the carpet. Jimmy hears Robson's strangled cry of frustration as they both see a dozen or so pieces of tape hanging inside the frame, each capable of securing a bag of narcotics. "Oh, Christ! How much shit do you suppose that joker took out of here?" Robson goes to the telephone, and soon the rooms are swarming with officers taking photographs and dusting for fingerprints. There is also a dog that sniffs around and becomes excited by the stereo system. The large speakers are ripped apart, revealing two plastic bags of white powder.

"Get that bozo up here," Robson orders. He prowls the room while waiting for the building manager to appear. When the man enters the apartment, he gasps at the disorder and nervously sits on the chair Robson has slammed down in the middle of the floor. "So what did you say your name is?" Robson begins.

"Cranley, Victor Cranley." Sweat appears at the edge of Cranley's receding hairline and dribbles down his forehead.

"Hm! Cranley . . . Hm! Mr. Victor Cranley." While repeatedly muttering the manager's name, Robson circles him. "Yes . . . Mr. Victor Cranley. Mr. Victor Cranley. Hm!" Jimmy sees Robson's performance is terrifying Cranley, who has no idea why he is being made to sit in the centre of a circle of hostile police officers. He turns his head, trying to follow Robson's movements.

Without warning, Robson snatches up one of the plastic bags and thrusts it at Cranley's face. Cranley recoils and almost tumbles backwards but for Jimmy, who moves forward to hold the chair. "Don't interfere, Mr. Sung!" Robson bellows at Jimmy, and then bends over until his big red face is almost touching Cranley's. "You see this bag, Mr. Victor Cranley? You see what's in it? You know what that stuff is, Mr. Victor Cranley? Do you?"

"No, sir . . . no. I don't," Cranley whispers.

Robson straightens up to look around at Jimmy and the officers in the room. "Would you believe it? Mr. Victor Cranley here says he doesn't know what this bag contains." The officers dutifully shake their heads in disbelief. "Do you guys actually think that Mr. Victor Cranley here, a man who probably spends hours sitting on his big ass looking at TV cop shows, doesn't have an itsy-bitsy clue what's in this bag? Now I ask you, isn't that a mite hard to believe?" The officers nod their heads in agreement. "Take a good look at the contents of this bag, Mr. Victor Cranley . . ." Robson shoves the bag into Cranley's face. "Take a real good look and make a guess what's in it."

Cranley, who is panting as if he has just run up a steep hill, finally says, "It could be drugs."

Robson now walks up to Cranley and pats his shoulder approvingly, while Cranley cringes like a dog expecting to be beaten. "Very good, Mr. Victor Cranley. Very good. This beautiful white stuff is cocaine. Now let me ask you, do you know anything about these two bags of shit being in this apartment?"

"No . . . no. I've never see them before." To Jimmy, it is obvious Cranley knows nothing but Robson needs someone on whom he can spill out his frustration. If Cranley were not so conveniently available, Jimmy thinks Robson might have struck out at one of his subordinates, or even at Jimmy.

"So, Mr. Victor Cranley, you weren't aware drugs were hidden in this apartment, is that correct?" Cranley shakes his head and the fat around his neck wobbles. "But somebody knew about it, right? And you . . ." Robson pokes a finger at Cranley's nose and the manager flinches away, trying to duck the accusatory rod. ". . . you, Mr. Victor Cranley, are the prize cocksucker who let that somebody into this apartment so he could collect the drugs and carry them away in a flight bag. Right?" Robson drops his voice to a stage whisper. "So what have you got to say for yourself, Mr. Victor Cranley?"

"I don't know what you mean," Cranley says.

"You don't!" bellows Robson. "Well, let me explain. I'm talking about that 'brother' of Martin MacDougail, the one you let into this apartment. Remember him? Remember how he left the apartment with a bag full of books?" Robson leans over until his nose almost touches Cranley's and whispers to him, "Mr. Cranley, I want you to listen carefully to what I'm going to say next. Are you listening, Mr. Cranley?" Cranley nods. "Martin MacDougail didn't have a brother." Robson straightens up and bellows, "Get it?" Cranley's mouth opens and closes. "Mr. Victor Cranley, you are now going to tell me exactly what the man you found so pleasant looked like . . . you are going to tell me what kind of aftershave lotion he used . . . whether he offered to suck you off . . . or vice versa." Robson's choice of words causes Cranley to close his eyes and moan. "And you're going to tell me these things real damn fast because you goddamn well know you should never have let that joker into this apartment in the first place."

Robson's performance leads Cranley to produce a description that would fit thousands of young men, including two of the police officers in the room. The only useful information Cranley offers is that the man spoke with a lisp. Robson tells Cranley he can leave, and Jimmy watches with sympathy as the exhausted apartment manager levers himself off the chair and staggers out of the room. Robson's behaviour has shamed and angered Jimmy, yet he cannot really fault Robson. After all, finding two small bags of cocaine is not much of a drug bust, especially when compared to what Robson might have found had he not been so quick to write off MacDougail's death as a suicide.

Soon Jimmy and Robson are standing in the street beside Robson's car. "There's something I've been wanting to ask you, Mr. Sung. Did Janet MacDougail tell you why she hired you instead of an experienced private investigator?" The implication that he does not have much of a professional reputation irritates Jimmy, but he masks his feeling and explains how it came about that Janet MacDougail selected his name from among others listed in the Yellow Pages. Robson shakes his head in wonderment at Janet's logic, and then asks Jimmy if he knows a good place to eat in Chinatown.

"Well, I go to Harry Lee's."

"Sounds fine to me," Robson says as he walks around his car and opens the door. "I'll follow you . . . for a change."

"Harry Lee's is nothing special."

"Just so long as the food's edible. And there's something I've been meaning to ask you . . . are you any relation to the big property-owner James Sung?"

"My uncle," Jimmy cautiously admits.

"Just curious. So, let's get going. And don't take long. I hate waiting for people."

Jimmy takes his time getting to the corner, but once there, quickens his stride and has difficulty preventing himself from running to the Corolla. He is irritated and wonders if Robson's insensitive, abrupt manner with him is beginning to cause feelings of racial inferiority, usually buried deep inside him, to come to the surface. He gets into the car and drives off, telling himself indulging in such pointless speculation will not get him any closer to the truth about Martin MacDougail. He rounds the corner, sounds the car horn and races on, hoping to lose Robson—but this does not happen. Each time Jimmy glances in his rear view mirror, there is Robson's car, right on his tail. Once on East Pender, Jimmy slows down, points at Harry Lee's Cafe, then drives on to park the Corolla in the back alley. He walks through Annette's store to find Robson and his mother engaged in a furious argument about Robson's right to park his car in the space Annette calls "her" loading zone.

"Suppose I get a delivery, eh? What then?" Annette is saying, as Jimmy joins them on the pavement.

"Tell the driver to go back into the alley to unload," Robson tells her. "Come on, let's go, Mr. Sung. I'm hungry."

"Here!" Annette gives Robson a large apple. "Apples are good for the skin and bowels."

Robson pockets the apple. "Thanks," he says, "though I don't give a damn anymore about my skin . . . and the other stopped functioning normally the day after I joined the police force. I'll give it to one of my kids." Robson takes Jimmy by the elbow and urges him along the street.

"Hey, wait a minute," Annette calls. "How many kids you got?"

Robson halts and tells her. "Two daughters. Eight and nine. Real cuties." Annette's response is to take a bag and fill it with apples.

"Here." She hands the bag to Robson. "Be sure to feed them plenty of apples, and don't forget the spinach either. Right? I've got the finest spinach in Vancouver."

"I'm sure you have, Mrs. Sung, I'm sure you have." Robson propels Jimmy on toward Harry Lee's cafe.

"Hey! What about moving your car?" Annette voice has become an indignant screech.

Robson halts and points a finger at Annette's sidewalk stands, which occupy over half the pavement. "I'll move my car when you move your produce stands back where they're supposed to be. Agreed?" Annette stares at Robson's back, speechless. Robson laughs as he and Jimmy turn to enter the cafe. "Your mother's quite the person. Is she always so feisty?"

"Always." The two men stand just inside the doorway, looking for a vacant table. Jimmy hears the words, "Over here, Nephew," and turns his head to see his uncle and Sam Mackintosh sitting at a corner table.

"There's my uncle with his friend. You want to sit with them?"

"Sure, why not?" They weave through the tables and Jimmy makes the introductions. Immediately Uncle Jimmy slips into the role of the dignified businessman in total control of the situation. That his uncle is a chameleon does not particularly surprise Jimmy, but Robson's transformation does. He suddenly becomes quiet, considerate, almost obsequious, and listens carefully as Uncle Jimmy speaks about downtown property development and city politics. At first Jimmy is at a loss to explain the change in Robson's manner, but eventually it dawns on him. Sergeant Robson has departed his own sphere of influence and entered the domain of his uncle's little empire; his uncle knows this and, more importantly, so does Robson, who is obviously prepared to pay his respects. Isn't it extraordinary, Jimmy thinks, how the ownership of property confers special status on individuals? Does this mean, he wonders, someone with title to a dilapidated dump in Vancouver's east side is more deserving of homage than someone who rents an expensive high rise apartment at English Bay? Given the extent of Uncle Jimmy's property holdings, it is easy to understand why Robson treats him with kid gloves.

Uncle Jimmy directs Harry Lee to bring more food. As soon as it arrives, Robson ravenously stuffs it into his mouth as though he has had nothing to eat for days. Between transferring food from his plate to his mouth, he asks Uncle Jimmy if he knows much about the MacDougail family.

"Let me see . . ." Uncle Jimmy stalls.

"Your nephew Jimmy is checking into the death of one of the family."

"Ah yes . . . *That* family. I hope my nephew is not making a nuisance of himself, Sergeant Robson."

"The contrary. I guess I'd have to say he's been of some help to us."

Uncle Jimmy produces a cluck, a compound sound of surprise and disbelief. "I'm delighted to hear that Nephew is becoming of use in the world. In the past he has behaved unintelligently and without direction."

Robson glances at Jimmy as Harry Lee lowers more dishes of food onto the table. "But getting back to the MacDougails . . ." Robson spoons large quantities of beef chow mein onto his plate. "It's beginning to look like Martin MacDougail was mixed up in drug trafficking." He drops his chopsticks and shouts at Harry Lee, "Hey, bring me a fork, will you?" He takes the fork and spears a large piece of broccoli. "You get the drift of what I'm saying, Mr. Sung?"

"Of course," Uncle Jimmy murmurs. "Did Nephew inform you what Sam here said about someone named MacDougail who occasionally visits Victory Square?"

"He did." Robson turns his head to look at Sam Mackintosh's alcohol-scored face, and Jimmy senses a hardening in Robson's manner. His uncle must have sensed it too, because he immediately makes it clear he will not allow Robson to put Sam through his verbal shredder. "Sam's an old, valued friend of mine," he says.

"Is that so," Robson replies. He fills his mouth with food and swallows before proceeding. "Mr. Mackintosh, sir, do you know this MacDougail?" Not too far behind his attempt at politeness lurks the police bully.

"Sort of," Sam says.

"Be a little more precise, Mr. Mackintosh."

"This guy showed up one day and I sort of got to know him."

"When was this?"

"A few years ago, I guess. Everybody calls him Mac."

"He's a boozer? Right?"

"That's about the cut of it," Sam agrees. "And he was never short of dough either."

"Hm!" Robson tilts a serving dish to scrape more food onto his plate. "So you really don't know much about this guy who might be named MacDougail. That right, Mr. Mackintosh?"

"That's about the cut of it," Sam agrees.

"Hm!" Robson turns to Uncle Jimmy "What about you, Mr. Sung? You know any people in the MacDougail family?" Jimmy notices a lessening of deference as Robson begins his questioning.

"I wouldn't say I knew them well. I am acquainted with people all around the world. But yes . . . I've chatted at different times with one or two of the family members. But I wouldn't classify them as friends."

"I'm not asking you to do that, Mr. Sung. I'm asking if you knew anyone in the family. For instance, did you know Martin MacDougail?"

"Definitely not. Any MacDougail I might know would be a person of my own generation."

"Then you know Martin MacDougail's grandmother?"

"I've met Mrs. MacDougail at the occasional social function. But you must appreciate, Sergeant Robson, that nowadays I don't mix much in Vancouver society."

"Neither does Mrs. MacDougail."

"What is the purpose of your line of questioning, Sergeant?"

"I was hoping to find out if you knew Martin's parents."

Uncle Jimmy appears to ruminate. "Just a moment . . . weren't they killed in an accident?"

"A boating accident," Jimmy supplements.

"Quite right, Nephew. A boating accident. I've always resisted owning or travelling on boats. They're prone to going underwater unexpectedly."

"Your fear of boats wouldn't have prevented you from meeting Martin's parents on dry land, would it?" Robson asks.

"I repeat, it's always possible I met his parents at some time or another."

"Don't forget Martin's parents are also the parents of Janet MacDougail, who is now employing your nephew to find out if her brother was pushed or jumped off the Lions Gate Bridge."

"Coincidence, Sergeant, mere coincidence. However, I am delighted my nephew is at last being employed by someone who presumably will pay him handsomely for his services."

Robson suddenly puts his fork down and stands. "Thanks, Mr. Sung, thanks for nothing. And you too, Mr. Mackintosh." He looks down at Jimmy and says, "I'll be in touch," before walking away from the table and out the restaurant door.

"What idiotic ideas are you hatching up, Nephew?" Uncle Jimmy asks. "Maybe it would be best if you confined your activities to collecting overdue debts and looking for runaway husbands and wives."

The comment riles Jimmy, who also stands. "Haven't you had enough experience to realize Sergeant Robson wouldn't be asking you questions unless he had good reason? And don't forget, there's a chance somebody has committed a murder, maybe even two."

"That's of no concern to me, Nephew."

"You beg the question, Uncle." Jimmy replies. "Before I leave, let me tell you something you ought to know. This afternoon I saw Robson working over a man about the same age as you, and it wasn't a pretty sight. So, if you or Sam do happen to know something significant about the MacDougail family, then I suggest you get in touch with Robson and tell him what it is before he finds out for himself and comes back looking for you."

On this note of high drama, Jimmy rings down the curtain on the scene, and stalks out of Harry Lee's.

That same evening Jimmy gets into the Corolla and drives to the MacDougail house with the intention of telling Janet and her grandmother Sergeant Robson has discovered drugs in Martin's apartment. He wants to get there before the police come to question them and maybe search the premises. Like other bearers of bad news, Jimmy is apprehensive he might be held responsible for the events he reports; but beyond that, he is worried he has become involved in something he is not qualified to handle. Reason tells him to withdraw from the investigation, but fear he will not see Janet again pulls him in the opposite direction. Even the possibility of not seeing her frightens him, and as he stops on the street outside the driveway to the MacDougail house, he attempts to quell the panic rapidly overtaking him. That Janet may feel nothing for him matters little—he is wholly consumed by his own feelings. He is profoundly shaken by the their depth, and dumbfounded to have fallen victim to emotions he used to laugh at when encountered in pop songs and movies-of-the-week.

Finally he drives up to the house and parks the car. When the unfriendly black-suited man, whose name Jimmy now knows is Beasley, answers the door, Jimmy tells him he wants to see Janet. Beasley responds by saying he will inform Mrs. MacDougail of Jimmy's arrival, and hurries to the sitting room. He returns and announces that Mrs. MacDougail will receive him.

Jimmy finds Mrs. MacDougail sitting in a chair, reading. She looks up as he approaches her. "I take it you've come here to tell me something, Mr. Sung." she says. "Is that correct?"

"I must speak to Janet first," Jimmy replies.

"I don't agree." Mrs. MacDougail places her book on a side table. "Well, what is it, Mr. Sung?"

Jimmy is exasperated but gives in, partly. He tells her about the cocaine found in Martin's apartment but says nothing about Betty Nelson. He concludes his narration by saying he wants to explain things to Janet. "I'm obligated to tell Janet what has happened. The news must be broken to her carefully."

"I'll assume what you tell me is accurate and verifiable, Mr. Sung. But I won't allow you to see Janet. I'll take care of that."

"But, Mrs. MacDougail—" Jimmy begins, puzzled that she does not appear concerned her grandson may have been using drugs.

"You were hired to make a limited investigation into my grandson's death in order to put Janet's mind at rest. It's regrettable the matter has got out of hand, but that being the case, Mr. Sung, we have no further need of your services." Mrs. MacDougail takes her book from the table, indicating that Jimmy is dismissed.

"But the police—" Jimmy begins, when the door opens and Janet enters. She has a towel wrapped around her head and is wearing a long, red, terrycloth bathrobe.

Janet stops when she sees Jimmy, then smiles and comes toward him, sidestepping the furniture, reminding Jimmy of a Greek goddess working her way around the statuary. "I've talked with Lucille, and we have decided you can drive her here Friday afternoon." Jimmy nods—like someone suffering from acute vertigo being asked to admire the view from the edge of a precipitous cliff, nodding his head is all he is capable of doing.

"Please leave us, Mr. Sung," Mrs. MacDougail orders.

"No, don't," cries Janet. "You've come to tell me something, Jimmy?" Jimmy nods and notices Janet's voice has risen and become childish. "There. You see, Gran? Jimmy doesn't have to go."

"You may not like what—" Jimmy begins.

"Mr. Sung!" Mrs. MacDougail's voice is strident. "Please go!"

"Granny!" Mrs. MacDougail hunches in her chair and seems to shrink in size. "I want to hear what Jimmy has to say. It's my money that's paying him." Janet smiles at Jimmy and her voice drops as she speaks to him. "It's all right, you can tell me," she says.

Jimmy licks his lips—the atmosphere in the room has evaporated the moisture in them. "Perhaps you were right . . . it's beginning to look as if Martin didn't commit suicide," he begins.

"There! You see?" Janet cries. "I told you it was an accident!"

"An accident remains a possibility, Janet," Jimmy begins again, unsure how to best to break the news, "but the police are beginning to think Martin may have been murdered. It appears your brother could have been involved in the narcotics trade."

"That is not true! You are lying to me." Janet's voice is childishly imperious. "Martin would never do anything like that."

"I'm afraid it may be true, Janet. The police found cocaine in his apartment."

"Somebody put it there to trap Martin," Janet categorically states. "Or friends asked Martin to keep it. Martin was always helping friends. He told me. Martin had millions of friends." She defies Jimmy to contradict her statements. "And you needn't worry about getting paid for your services. I have plenty of money. Tell Gran how much I owe you, and she'll give you a cheque right now, won't you, Gran?" Janet turns and quickly leaves the room, watched by a despairing Jimmy.

"Satisfied, Mr. Sung?" Mrs. MacDougail inquires, but Jimmy, who feels like grabbing and hurling pieces of furniture around the room, does not answer. Instead, he hurries out and is about to fling open the front door when he hears his name being whispered. He turns, sees Janet sitting at the landing on the stairs and crosses the hall to look up at her.

"Is it really true about Martin?" she asks.

"I'm afraid so." Jimmy climbs the stairs and sits beside her. "I'm very sorry."

"But why would Martin hide cocaine in his apartment?"

"I don't know."

"I didn't mean to be nasty to you," Janet tells him.

"You're upset." Jimmy takes her hand and pats it, a familiar gesture, one frequently used by Lucille when she seeks reconciliation following a bout of tigerish fury directed at Jimmy.

"I like you patting my hand. Sometimes I need somebody to tell me I haven't done anything wrong."

"What nonsense. I'm sure you haven't done too many wrong things in your life."

"You'd be surprised. Sometimes I tell Gran fibs."

"Everyone tells an occasional fib," Jimmy reassures her. "Lucille tells them by the dozen."

"But that's different. Lucille's beautiful, and our art teacher says beauty excuses all faults."

"Well then, if you have any faults they're excused too."

"You're nice."

"I'm really sorry I wasn't able to bring good news."

She sighs. "Do you think Martin was selling drugs to that girl I saw him talking to on the street?"

For a moment Jimmy wonders how Janet can so readily accept her brother's involvement with drugs. Does it suggest she already knows something? But Jimmy remains cautious; he does not want to say anything he may later regret. "I really know very little about narcotics." he says, while feeling sympathy for what Janet must be going through. He supposes she must be devastated at the thought Martin might have been corrupting girls her own age.

Janet leans against him to rest her head on his shoulder. "It's awful when you find out something horrible about a person you've always admired. You wonder how he can do such things."

"You mean like selling drugs?" Janet moves her head, and Jimmy can see she is not looking at him. Her eyes are focused on something beyond, on some remembered image she finds repulsive. "Don't blame yourself for what your brother did," Jimmy says, anxious to comfort her.

"Should I have known about the bad things Martin was doing?"

"How could you? People don't talk about that kind of thing." Jimmy remembers the photographs of naked children in Martin's apartment.

"Do you keep things to yourself?" she asks.

"Some things."

"But you wouldn't ever sell drugs to a girl like Lucille, would you?"

"I couldn't."

She sighs and Jimmy, watching her, begins to feel as though he's floating in space. "Do I look unhappy?" she asks.

"Melancholy."

This seems to please her. "I expect I'll feel melancholy for a long time. Maybe Lucille won't want to be friends any more. She probably doesn't like people who are sad."

"That won't make any difference to Lucille. She likes you."

"Most people start out liking me," Janet says, "but end up dropping me." Although Jimmy feels uncomfortable with the idea, nevertheless he is coming to the conclusion that Janet is a perfect example of the "poor little rich girl" syndrome. She probably has no idea what goes on beyond her walled-in-by-money world. Maybe he should remind her (but he doesn't) that her present unhappiness is minuscule compared to what some girls her age experience, like those who stand in the streets peddling their bodies. He also considers pointing out (but elects not to do so) that the financial security her family provides cannot help but alleviate any discomfort she might experience from time to time due to unpleasant memories of her dead brother. "I wish I had somebody like Lucille to live with me," she says. "We have lots in common." Maybe that is true, Jimmy thinks; perhaps Janet and Lucille could be happy living together. He knows spontaneous friendships do form between people, especially teenaged girls. His own teenage years he recalls as being emotionally dead. He absent-mindedly strokes Janet's hand while speculating on the effect his abnormal adolescence may have had upon his development as an adult. Janet sighs. "Maybe if our parents hadn't died when we were so young, Martin might have turned out differently." She sighs again, and rearranges the towel around her damp hair. "Do you have any ideas yet about who murdered Martin?"

Janet's question surprises Jimmy, and after a pause he tells her he thinks maybe the police will never discover the actual circumstances of Martin's death. He does not mention the man with the lisp who came to Martin's apartment, nor does he describe his visit to the house in East Vancouver or what happened to Betty Nelson.

"But that police officer you were with in Martin's apartment, does he think Martin was murdered?"

"He thinks it's probable, but at the moment there's no evidence to prove it."

"But you can find out if Martin was murdered, and who did it," Janet tells him. "You're smarter than the police." At this point Jimmy knows he should tell Janet of his intention to remove himself from the investigation, but finds he cannot do it, especially after Janet starts to cry. He puts his arms around her, becoming aware of the shape and movement of her breasts shifting under the red terrycloth. "I'll do what I can," he tells her, "but you mustn't be disappointed if I don't get results."

"You will . . . you must. I want to know what really happened." She sits closer to Jimmy, like an unhappy child seeking comfort. Jimmy wants to ease Janet's unhappiness, but at the same time he cannot prevent himself from enjoying the sexual sensations aroused in him by the movements of her body. He is quite prepared to sit here beside Janet for the rest of his life.

"I suppose I'll eventually recover from Martin's death. But it's bound to take a while," she says.

"You'll be fine," Jimmy tells her.

They sit in companionable silence for a time, and then Janet totally astonishes him by saying, "Maybe I could help your mother out in the store. It might be fun."

Jimmy cannot believe Janet could actually think bagging fruit and vegetables for twelve hours a day could be a pleasant activity. "It's hard work," he says. "You're on your feet all day."

Jimmy doubts whether Janet even hears him. "I might even learn some Chinese. I know a bit of French, but I'm not really good at languages. I'm no good at anything." Recalling her academic limitations makes Janet lugubrious again, and Jimmy wonders if she is on the verge of crossing the divide between genuine sadness and histrionic self-pity. (Jimmy is quite familiar with this condition; he often encounters it in himself and in his sisters, especially Lucille.)

"Nonsense," he briskly informs her. "You're intelligent . . . and brave," he adds, finding it hard to believe all his years of education have not enabled him to produce anything more profound.

"You say that because you are a kind person," she whimpers, determined to deny herself any redeeming qualities. "I don't get good grades at school."

Jimmy wonders how failure to get high marks in school could make an iota of difference in the life of someone like Janet MacDougail. Why, not so very long ago, most females of her age were balanced on the fulcrum of life; those who remained unmarried beyond this point had no choice but to plod the dreary road to spinsterhood. Once Jimmy had read—where was it?—that girls are capable of love and sexual gratification long before boys are; hadn't he read in his literature course at university tales from *The Decameron* in which girls Janet's age and younger avidly pursue and embrace adult male lovers? And what about that snippet of information he had come across, in which Mark Twain—of all people—had concluded that women are more fortunate than men because women are able to enjoy making love from eight years to eighty? Wouldn't it be preferable for Janet to be given an opportunity to revel in passionate love affairs instead of having to worry about getting into university?

"Maybe I'll skip school tomorrow," Janet says and moves along the landing, out of Jimmy's encircling arm. "I don't want to be there if that awful police officer shows up. I'd be so embarrassed." She leans over, removes a slipper and scratches her toes, which Jimmy cannot help noticing are long and bony, so unlike Lucille's short, plump ones.

"Do you have relatives in Vancouver where you can stay?"

"I suppose. There's Aunt Mary on my mother's side of the family." She replaces the slipper and yawns. It seems to Jimmy that she inclines towards him, and he leans forward to kiss her cheek. But she draws back to look intently at him. "Do you still love me? You haven't changed your mind?" she asks, and Jimmy nods his head, first yes, then no, all the while condemning himself for his muteness. Janet stands and looks down at him. "That's good," she says. She smiles, removes the towel from around her head, and goes up the stairs with the still damp towel trailing behind.

Thus is the object of Jimmy's love eclipsed, and he remains seated on the landing feeling like a terrible fool. Who but a fool, he thinks, would fall in love with a seventeen-year-old schoolgirl? Who but a fool would have allowed himself to be dragged into a series of skits in which the audience laughs uproariously as he (a former whiz kid) experiences one humiliation after another? This could only have happened, he concludes, because he is the sort of person destined to do the right thing at the wrong time, who can be counted on to show up at a funeral with a bottle of champagne or at a wedding dressed in black. Yes, it is true, he tells himself, I am fated to reverse things. Perhaps that explains why U.J. accuses me of being grossly deficient in common sense, which he says is an essential ingredient for me to possess in order to safely transport myself through life without experiencing any major mishaps on the way. Though, as Jimmy now sits on the landing in the

MacDougail house thinking about U.J.'s lectures on the subject of common sense, he cannot understand how what seems (to him) such a scarce commodity—that is, sense—can be so plentifully distributed among human beings that U.J. can call it common.

Jimmy is still sitting on the landing when Beasley crosses the hall a few minutes later and spots him. "Don't worry," Jimmy says, "I'm leaving." And he does. He moves quickly down the stairs, passes Beasley, who is standing in the middle of the hall, opens the front door and then slams it, hoping its hinges will spring and the house will come tumbling down. Of course, that doesn't happen, because it is only in Jimmy's world houses (and sometimes lives) collapse when people angrily depart from them.

◆   ◆   ◆

The next morning when Annette and Jimmy arrive to open the store they find Janet sitting on the curb. When she tells them she has not eaten anything, Jimmy quickly volunteers to buy her breakfast at Harry Lee's. His uncle and Sam Mackintosh are there too, drinking coffee.

"Sam and I are on our way out to Langley to look over some colts," Uncle Jimmy remarks after they are seated at his table. He turns to Janet. "You must be the young lady I've heard so much about."

"You and Jimmy have the same names," Janet remarks.

Uncle Jimmy closes his eyes. "That's quite true, my dear. It's a grey cloud hanging over my head that can never be dispersed."

"I don't think having a nephew with the same name is so horrible, Mr. Sung. Besides, Jimmy's a nice person. He's helped me a lot."

At this point Harry Lee comes to the table and Uncle Jimmy orders breakfast without consulting with anybody about what they want. Once it is served Janet tells the men she usually does not eat breakfast. "I hate to get out of bed in the morning, so most days I'm late getting up and don't have time for breakfast."

"I wouldn't get up early either if I were in your bed," Uncle Jimmy says in Mandarin. Loathing for his uncle infuses Jimmy. How dare U.J. project lecherous images of Janet awakening in her bed? Of course similar images constantly flicker through Jimmy's mind, but then he loves Janet.

After they have finished eating, Jimmy tells Janet it is time to leave. "I'll take care of the bill," Uncle Jimmy says. "Some people can't afford to purchase meals for others." In the street, when Janet asks if it is true he is poor, he angrily says, "Listen, what my uncle says is a lot of nonsense." Jimmy wants to use stronger words but is afraid he will offend Janet.

"Then why would your uncle say something like that?"

The dam in Jimmy bursts, and pent-up resentment floods out. "Because he enjoys baiting me in front of other people," he storms. "He's a sadistic swine, a hypocritical little banana."

Janet immediately turns back to the cafe entrance. "I'm going back to tell him off," she says.

"Please don't. It would only make matters worse. Anyway, I hardly ever see him." He leads Janet away from the cafe. "Though for some reason, lately he's been around a lot."

"Your uncle sort of reminds me of Gran. She thinks she can say anything she likes to me. I know she loves me, but sometimes I get mad at her. You know something, Jimmy? You and your uncle sort of look alike." Jimmy does not respond, and by now they have reached the entrance to Annette's store. Janet goes over to Annette, who wraps her in a green apron, while Jimmy goes upstairs to his office.

There he sits, trying to make sense of what he knows about Martin MacDougail, comparing himself to a person attempting to complete a jigsaw puzzle with half the pieces missing. He asks himself what sort of people would likely be hovering in the shadows behind Martin, assuming he was dealing drugs. Admittedly, Jimmy knows little or nothing about trafficking in narcotics but figures it must work like any other profitable business operation, which needs working capital, managerial expertise and human resources that can be readily moved around the world and blended invisibly into the social and economic network of a community. So where in Canada would you find these ingredients? For Jimmy, the answer readily comes. You would find them in large urban centres, especially port cities. Yes, in places like Vancouver where it would be easy enough to infiltrate legitimate businesses, even professional groups. But where would someone like Martin MacDougail slot in? Middle management? Surely not. Local distributor? Probably. That is, until one day he decides to go into business for himself and sidetracks a shipment of cocaine, for which he gets killed. Yes, Jimmy thinks, it's a framework that makes sense. He is pleased with his theory, yet uncomfortably aware that it is beyond his meagre resources to gather the evidence to prove it.

◆　　◆　　◆

Jimmy is amazed when he answers the telephone and hears Robson's voice. "It's just as I expected. The grandmother says she knows nothing about Martin's drug dealing."

"You think she's telling the truth?" Jimmy asks.

"My guess is she knows a helluva lot, but there's not much I can do to get it out of her." Robson's call is a breakthrough for Jimmy; the information he supplies Jimmy about Mrs. MacDougail has been tacked onto his question to Jimmy concerning the whereabouts of Janet. Robson laughs when Jimmy tells him Janet is helping Annette in the store and says he will drop by later in the afternoon to ask the girl a few questions.

"Like what?" Jimmy's first reaction is to protect her.

"Oh, only suitable questions." Robson is in good humour. "You know the sort of thing—like when did you last have sex and where." His rattling laugh jars in Jimmy's ear. "You think Janet's as innocent as my little kids, don't you, Mr. Sung?"

"I know nothing about your children, Sergeant, and I have no idea why you raise the subject now."

"I'm merely suggesting you should be more cautious

about assessing people at face value, especially a girl with a body like that."

"What can you know about Janet? You haven't questioned her yet."

"So I'll find out more this afternoon. Right?"

"Wait a minute," Jimmy angrily replies. "You never once questioned Janet about her brother's death, but now you're hinting—"

"I never hint. I deal strictly in facts."

Jimmy tries to pin Robson down. "Do you know where Martin got the cocaine?"

"Who knows? He might have stolen it. Or he might have been peddling it for someone else."

"But you have no idea who the supplier is?"

"It could be you, Mr. Sung . . . or your uncle and his sidekick, Mr. Mackintosh."

"Oh, come off it, Sergeant."

"You think I'm being ridiculous? That's only because you're like a newborn when it comes to the narcotics trade, Mr. Sung. I'm telling you, whoever Martin was working with could be any one of your average, hard-working, tax-paying citizens. Just remember that photo album of naked kids, Mr. Sung. Guys like you'd be surprised at what goes on in this city." He hangs up, leaving Jimmy all the more uneasy about the prospect of Robson questioning Janet.

◆　　◆　　◆

At one o'clock Janet appears and asks Jimmy to take her for lunch; Jimmy, only too pleased to oblige, squires her to a Chinese restaurant located in one of the few buildings in the area not owned by his uncle. The waitress is disgusted when Jimmy orders beef fried noodles for Janet and soup for himself instead of the daily special, which is octopus. "Don't you know a good deal when you see one? Are you stupid or something?" she says and stumps off to place the order.

"What did she say?" Janet wants to know.

"She said we chose well because the octopus tastes like bicycle tires."

"Oh."

Once the food arrives, Jimmy carefully arranges Janet's fingers around the chopsticks and watches while she noisily sucks noodles through pursed lips. As she eats, Jimmy tries to elicit information about her family, but Janet says there is nothing to tell. When Jimmy remarks that he can understand why Janet's grandmother is so protective of her, Janet agrees. "Gran doesn't want anything bad to happen to me." She suddenly asks, "Do you love your sisters?"

Jimmy, spoon raised over the serving dish, pauses. Do his feelings for Julia and Lucille qualify as love? While he realizes what he feels for his sisters bears no resemblance to his feelings for Janet, yet, as he brings to mind Julie's affectionate nature and Lucille's beauty and considers how impossible it is for him to imagine his life without them, he decides he must love them. "Yes, I do love them," he answers, "though they're so much a part of my life I've never thought of my feelings for them as love. Why do you ask?"

"I . . . wondered . . . if you would ever hurt them. Would you?"

"What do you mean? In what way?" Jimmy sees that for some reason Janet is impatient with him, as if he ought immediately to understand her question. "Do you mean, have I ever physically abused my sisters?" Janet avoids his question, so Jimmy suggests she ask his sisters their opinion of him.

"I couldn't do that," she quickly says.

"Why not? They wouldn't object." Then, presuming a reason for Janet's question, he asks, "Did Martin abuse you?"

An expression of horror momentarily appears on her face. "No. No . . . Martin was kind to me." Jimmy thinks he detects a false note, but is not sure. He tries to think of a way to frame a question he would like to ask Janet about her relationship with Martin but, as though aware of his intent, she disconcerts him by smiling brilliantly and changing the subject.

"Being here in this restaurant makes me feel grown-up," she announces. "Do I look older? I think I've grown up a little . . . become a bit more mature . . . since Martin died. How old are you, Jimmy?"

This is a question Jimmy does not want to answer. But since it has been directly posed, he feels he can neither avoid it or lie, and so he finally says, "Twenty-seven."

Janet smiles as she slips a piece of beef between her lips. "Martin was younger. When I was a child I always looked up to him because he was older than me, and could do things I didn't know how to do."

"Such as?" Jimmy asks, experiencing intense jealousy.

"Why are you always asking me questions?"

"I suppose because I want to know details—I have trouble accepting blanket statements. And don't forget, you did ask me to help you find out how Martin died."

"Oh that! That doesn't matter."

"What do you mean, doesn't matter?"

"Helping me doesn't matter anymore."

"I don't understand what you're getting at," Jimmy says, while Janet lowers her eyes and watches him through the veil of her lashes.

"Nothing," she finally says, and then asks, "Do you still . . . love me ?"

"You must know I do, so why ask?"

"I suppose because nobody has ever told me they love me." Janet seems puzzled by something. "How does a person know when she loves somebody?"

"You just know."

She looks down at her plate again. "If you love somebody, does that mean you want to . . . you know?"

"I suppose so."

Janet now stirs what is left of the food on her plate. "Have you ever done that?" Her head is turned and she watches Jimmy obliquely.

"Yes."

She hesitates before saying, "I don't really understand

that sort of thing. Does it mean there might be something wrong with me?"

"No. When I was your age I didn't know anything about sex either."

"Do you think Lucille knows?"

"You should ask her."

"Oh no. I could never do that." She sighs. "Maybe you'll stop loving me. That happened to me. I found I couldn't love Martin any more. It made me feel bad, but there was nothing I could do about it."

"What was your reason for not loving him any more?"

Once again Janet lowers her eyes. "I don't know," she says as she shrugs and gives a little laugh. "I guess it just happened."

"I'm hoping you'll eventually come to love me," Jimmy bravely declares.

"I don't suppose I ever will," she says. "I don't even love Gran."

Jimmy manages a tepid smile, although he is so upset by Janet's rejection he wants to jump up and run out of the restaurant. "Maybe we should talk about other things," he says. "Perhaps you could tell me more about yourself."

"But I don't want to. I get frightened when people ask me questions."

"Then perhaps we should go back to the store, unless you'd like something more to eat," he says.

"No, thank you. It was very nice." Jimmy has noticed Janet classifies experiences as either "nice" or "bad," and now he wonders if these expressions are of class origin. At least they are not as irritating as "right on" and "the pits" or worse, "radical" and "really gross."

Janet waits by the door while Jimmy pays the bill. Then, as they stroll towards the store, she reaches out to clasp his hand. For Jimmy, it is as though she has reached out and touched his heart. "We could go for a walk," he suggests. He feels he could walk with Janet until they dropped to the earth and died.

"I'd like that," she responds.

But Jimmy remembers Robson is coming to interview Janet later in the afternoon, and he readjusts to the exigencies of the investigation. "We'll go this evening. Down to the harbour to look at the ships. We can chose the one we'd like to sail away on." He is unable to prevent himself from wishing for the impossible.

Annette is standing on the pavement talking to a customer as they approach the store. She eyes their clasped hands. "What did I tell you, Jimmy," she says in Mandarin when they reach her. "She took your hand, didn't she? I know she did, because you'd be too scared to take hers."

"What did you say?" Janet asks.

"I said this business doesn't run to two-hour lunches," Annette replies, as Janet excuses herself and clatters upstairs towards the toilet. "What did I tell you, Jimmy!" Annette crows. "What did I tell you?"

Jimmy wonders if he will ever find a way to squash his mother's futile hopes for his future status as husband of Janet MacDougail. What can he do to make his mother aware of the enormous barriers that prevent marriage between them? Jimmy has never thought of Annette as being sentimental—she has always personified solid reality—but, as he stands on the pavement looking at his mother, for the first time he understands that romanticism is an integral part of her personality. He grasps that almost everything his mother does, even down to the manner in which she arranges produce for sale in her market, is coloured by a romantic dream she has of herself and her children. Isn't it strange, Jimmy thinks, that he has lived with this woman for twenty-seven years and yet knows so little about her inner life? This revelation disturbs him. It reveals something he was not aware of before this moment, the extent of his own blindness in perceiving the true nature of the people with whom he supposes he has intimate relationships.

When Janet returns, Annette ties the strings of the green apron around her waist and puts her to work sweeping the floor. Jimmy remains a few minutes watching Janet busy herself around the store, then goes upstairs to his office, where he stands at the window to dream of the wondrous flowers of passion that quite miraculously begin to bloom when two people fall in love with each other.

7

"**H**ello there, Mrs. Sung! I notice your display stands are still halfway across the pavement. Like I told you before—it's a violation of city bylaws."

Jimmy awakens from his daydream to the sound of Sergeant Robson's bombastic reproval and his mother's indignant protests. By the time he catapults from his chair and dashes down the stairs and into the store, Robson is already chatting with Janet. "Hi there, Mr. Sung," he says as Jimmy appears and tells him he can use the upstairs office to talk to Janet privately.

"That's fine with me," Robson says, personifying cooperation itself. He smiles at Janet. "I think Ms. MacDougail may be upset with me because I didn't listen to what she had to say before. That right, Ms. MacDougail? Well, let's see if we can't set the record straight. Lead the way to your office, Mr. Sung. I'm all ears."

"Don't keep her too long," Annette calls.

"Just a few hours, Mrs. Sung." Robson laughs, although his ponderous humour does not sit well with Annette, who sniffs and pats nearby ginger roots and savoy cabbages.

"Hm!" Robson looks around the dingy little room. "So this is where you conduct business, eh Mr. Sung? Hm! Very impressive." Janet sits in the chair reserved for clients, and Robson perches on Jimmy's desk in such a way Jimmy is forced to move his chair to one side in order to see Janet and at the same time keep an eye on Robson. Jimmy notices Janet appears nervous and wonders why, because he is certain she cannot tell Robson anything he doesn't already know. Robson commences by offering reassurance. "You don't have to worry about my questions, Ms. MacDougail."

"I'm not worried," Janet replies, although there is a tremor in her voice, which Jimmy is sure Robson notices.

"I'll butt in if necessary. Okay?" Jimmy says.

Robson turns to look at Jimmy. "You'll stay out of this discussion, Mr. Sung. Right out." He glares at Jimmy for a few seconds, then swings back to Janet. "You have relatives in Seattle, Ms. MacDougail?"

The question startles Janet. After a moment she replies, "Yes . . . I do."

"Many?"

"Three cousins. They're older than me."

"In their twenties? Thirties?"

"I suppose. I don't really know."

"Does one of your cousins have a lisp?"

"None of them lisps," Janet states firmly.

"Well, then . . ." Robson continues. "Have you ever met anyone with a lisp?" Janet turns her head and looks at the wall. "Take your time," Robson encourages.

"I don't remember if I have."

"Think it over for a minute or two." Robson stares at Jimmy, forbidding him to interfere.

"I may have," she finally says.

"I see. Could this person have been someone acquainted with your cousins?"

"I don't know," Janet says.

"Let me explain something, Ms. MacDougail." Jimmy cannot believe Robson is the same man who brutally questioned Victor Cranley: this man seems to possess endless patience. "My job is to sort out things. That's what detectives do. So when something happens—an accident, or a crime—and

I'm asked to investigate it, the first thing I do is sort out the people, who they are, what they do, how they're related to each other. And that means asking questions. Some of them may not seem to make sense at first, even to me. But later, if I can make connections that provide explanations, they don't seem so silly after all. See what I mean?"

Janet nods and tells Robson she is sorting through her memories to check if she has ever encountered anyone with a lisp.

"Good. Take your time."

"I may have met somebody like that once."

"Hm. Was this at your home?"

"Oh, no. Gran would never allow a man like that into our house."

There follows a pause, during which Jimmy senses a change in Robson, a slight hardening in his approach. "What you mean 'a man like that'?"

Robson's question seems to embarrass Janet, who turns her head away as she answers. "Somebody who looks at girls . . . you know . . . in a certain way."

"When you say 'in a certain way', Ms. MacDougail, what're you referring to?" Robson's voice is neutral.

Janet stares at her hands. "He was thinking . . . things . . . about me."

"I see," Robson murmurs. "He wasn't a pleasant sort of guy, is that what you mean?"

"I didn't think so."

"So where did you meet this man?"

"I'm not sure."

"Was it with your brother? Or your cousins?"

"I don't remember. Aren't you going to ask me anything about Martin?"

"Presently, Ms. MacDougail, presently. But right now I want to know more about your other relatives. You've told me about your cousins in Seattle, and I appreciate that. Now let's consider some other places. What about San Francisco and Los Angeles? You have any relatives living there?"

"Yes," she sullenly replies.

"Do they come to visit you and your grandmother?"

"They come to see Granny. Why do you want to know?"

"Remember what I told you about detectives asking questions?" Janet nods, but Jimmy detects a change in her demeanour: she has become cautious. "Do you ever go visit your relatives?"

"Sometimes. Gran doesn't like to fly. It makes her ankles swell."

"Do you ever go on your own?"

"Yes, but it's boring. I go because Gran makes me."

"But surely travelling around North America couldn't be so terribly boring. I understand you also have family in the eastern United States and Canada."

Janet becomes haughty. "Who I visit is none of your business. Anyway, I expect everybody visits relatives."

"Yes, that's true. Even I visit relatives from time to time." Harmless geniality radiates from Robson as he continues asking seemingly innocuous questions about Janet's family visits. Although Jimmy tries to prevent it happening, he finds himself picturing a flawlessly constructed, intricately woven, inconspicuous criminal network through which a young girl might move without danger of discovery.

Robson shifts his line of questioning back to Martin. "Did your brother bring friends to the house?"

"He did before he got his own apartment."

"But you were able to give Mr. Sung a list of your brother's friends, weren't you?"

Janet's eyelids rapidly flutter and she swallows several times. "That's because Martin told me about them."

Robson now pulls the list out of his pocket and puts it on the desk, while Janet looks indignantly at Jimmy, who manages an apologetic smile. "The reason I mention the list, Ms. Mac-Dougail, is that my officers have checked it out, but weren't able to match these names with people at the university."

Janet raises her head and stares at the ceiling. "I expect they didn't look hard enough."

"That's possible," Robson agrees. "However, when an officer went to your school and looked through your class yearbook he had no trouble finding students with the same names as those on the list."

"I have no idea what you're talking about."

"Let me tell you, Ms. MacDougail, what I think has happened. Mr. Sung asks you for the names of your brother's friends. You want to help him, so you promise to give him a list. But there's a little problem, which is that you don't actually know the names of any of Martin's friends. So, because you don't want to disappoint Mr. Sung, you give him names of girls at your school. The officer found the girls whose names you listed, Ms. MacDougail, but none of them knew your brother. See what I mean? You mustn't try to be too helpful." For a moment Janet looks directly at Jimmy, admission in her eyes, then returns to looking at the ceiling. "Did Martin ever talk about a woman named Betty?"

"No."

"I see. Now, you told Mr. Sung your brother visited you on the Saturday."

"Yes . . . in the evening. He came in by the side door so Gran wouldn't know."

"Why didn't Martin want your grandmother to see him?"

"Gran thought he drank too much."

"Was Martin drinking that night?"

"He may have been."

"Have you any idea what time it was when Martin visited you?"

"I don't know. I was reading in bed."

"Could it have been as late as ten or eleven o'clock?"

"Maybe."

"Were you surprised your brother came so late?"

"No. Sometimes he'd wake me in the middle of the night."

"Really," Robson mildly comments. "Now, getting back to the man with the lisp. You can't remember when or where you saw him?"

"No."

Robson gets up, walks to the window, looks out for a minute or so, then returns to the desk. "I want to tell you something I've noticed about my daughters, Ms. MacDougail. Have I told you I have two girls, eight and nine?" Janet shakes her head. "Now, there's something I've noticed when my girls talk to me about people they like or dislike—they tell me what the people say to them, but they never say anything about how they look at them. See what I'm getting at?" Janet nods and Robson smiles at her. "I don't want to embarrass you, Ms. Mac-Dougail, but it's important for me to know more about the man with the lisp. You're seventeen years old, about ten years older than my daughters. You're a young woman, not a girl, right? And as a young woman you're aware of how some men look at women, to use your words, 'in a certain way'. Right? So when I add this all up, it makes me think you saw the man with the lisp fairly recently, and that being so, it's not unreasonable to expect you to be able to remember where and when this happened."

"Sergeant—" Jimmy begins.

"Keep quiet, Mr. Sung," Robson barks. He turns to Janet. "Well?"

"It was some time ago. I don't remember where."

Robson shrugs his shoulders. "Okay. We'll leave it at that. But please think about it, and if you remember anything, tell Mr. Sung and he'll pass along the information." Robson walks Janet to the door and courteously opens it for her. "Oh, something you should know. A bunch of TV cameramen and reporters are hanging around your house, so why don't you ask Mrs. Sung to put you up for the night?"

As Robson shows Janet out, Jimmy glances at his watch and notes it is twenty minutes to four on the afternoon of his weekly four o'clock visit to Evelyn Chan.

Robson makes sure the door is firmly closed and returns to stand beside the desk. "So, what's your reaction, Mr. Sung? You believe what she said?"

"Why shouldn't I?" Jimmy cautiously replies.

"You must be even more simple-minded than I thought. Though what puzzles me is why she's lying."

"Janet has no reason to lie."

"That's what I just said. There's no reason, so why do it?"

"She may have a poor memory."

"Or a convenient one."

"The fact you weren't able to match people to the names on Janet's list doesn't mean the people don't exist."

"Forget it. The girl's lying. And I intend to find out why."

"The drug connection is what puzzles me," Jimmy says. "Surely you see that Janet can't be mixed up in that."

"Hey, selling drugs's not all that different from delivering newspapers, except the pay's better and you don't have to get up so early in the morning. And there's no age restriction either. In fact, the younger you are, the faster you catch on to the basic facts of our free enterprise system."

"But what about Betty Nelson and the house on the east side? Where do they fit in?" says Jimmy as they move toward the door.

"Well, we've established that Betty Nelson died of a heroin overdose, though traces of seconal were also found in her blood. And we know she lived in an apartment in Kitsilano. But we found nothing of interest there, only the usual stuff plus some college texts and notebooks." Robson begins to open the door.

"But Janet's not mixed up in any of that, right?"

"I never rule anything out until the case file is closed, Mr. Sung." Robson shuts the door and leans against it. "Hm! I've been doing some checking on Janet's parents. Want to hear what happened to them?"

"They drowned?"

"No. They were going out in their boat for the weekend when it exploded, minutes after moving away from the wharf."

"Janet told me there had been some sort of accident."

"There's something else you might find of interest: an investigation into drug trafficking around Vancouver was going on at the time of the explosion. And what's more, two MacDougails were among the people questioned. One was Janet's father, the other's the guy Sam Mackintosh says he knows. Interesting stuff, eh?"

"But it doesn't prove Janet knew anything about Martin's involvement with drugs."

"Want to lay a bet?"

"I'm sure she knows nothing," Jimmy manages to say, and it irks him to hear himself utter such a tepid denial.

"Never rule anybody out, Mr. Sung. You sure it's okay with your mother to have the girl around the store?"

"Mother likes her."

"That's understandable. There's a big pile of money sitting underneath her."

The insinuation makes Jimmy furious and it shows. "Is it impossible for you to grasp that Janet is a very nice girl, someone people actually like?"

Robson closes the door, and once more leans against it. "Sure, she's nice. But y'know something, Mr. Sung, I've put away some real nice people in my time, and some of the nicest ones turned out to be the biggest crooks. So let me put a question to you, Mr. Sung—what's so goddamn wonderful about being nice?"

This time Robson opens the door wide. "And don't relay anything I've told you to Janet MacDougail. That would be very unwise. Okay?" He goes out and closes the door.

Jimmy stands at the window a moment or two, waiting for Robson to drive off. As he moves toward the door there is a tap on it, and Janet comes in. At once, she wants to know why Robson asked her about her relatives. And what can Jimmy reply? Should he tell Janet that wherever she goes from now on she is likely to be followed and closely observed? That if she travels to visit relatives her luggage may be side-tracked and searched? Envisaging these things happening to Janet frightens Jimmy because he believes—in fact, he is sure—Janet is innocent of any wrongdoing. But suppose she is unknowingly acting as a courier? What then? Jimmy sees her being stripped, immodestly searched and physically humiliated by narcotics agents as brutal and relentless in their pursuit of drug traffickers as the dealers themselves are in pushing their products across borders and onto city streets. But surely Janet's family would never place her in such jeopardy. And yet, who exactly is Janet's family? Mrs. MacDougail? And what kind of a woman is she? Jimmy's encounters with her have left him confused and humiliated, and even with Janet he often feels he is being condemned for failing to see something which has been long apparent to other people. He compares himself to a parent who, upon being told that a pleasant, trusted neighbour has been sexually abusing children in the neighbourhood, finds he cannot bring himself to believe the man with whom he has been chatting for years over the backyard fence has actually committed these terrible acts. And because the realization of the neighbour's wrongdoing is beyond the parent's grasp, he harshly condemns himself because this suggests he is not capable of protecting his own children from abuse by others. Jimmy now experiences a similar contempt for himself; he suspects he is being manipulated, although he is not sure by whom or for what reason. He wants to question Janet further, but his love for her drains him of all resolution.

Janet stands close to Jimmy as she says, "Did Sergeant Robson say anything about me? Does he believe me?" Beyond the scent of fruit and vegetables that impregnates the green apron, Jimmy can discern the warm odours of Janet's body and the fragrance of the soap she uses. "You believe me, don't you?"

"Of course. But Robson needs to locate the man who got into Martin's apartment. The manager—Cranley is his name—told Robson the man had a lisp."

"Oh . . ." She breathes the word out. "I only saw him for a few minutes."

"I know. But it establishes a link with Martin."

"He was standing with Martin in front of the house, beside Martin's car, one day when I went outside."

"Why didn't you tell Robson?"

"Because I don't want to think about the guy . . . about the way he looked at me." Janet's face becomes flushed. "It was so embarrassing."

"I understand how you felt, but you must tell Robson

about this. If you don't, I'll have to. I can't withhold information from the police."

"I don't know why you insist on telling that stupid sergeant everything you find out. You can always just forget it."

"I can't. I'm a lawyer and an officer of the court."

"Why are you being nasty to me? You are acting like he does."

"Janet, I'm doing everything I can to help you."

"You aren't." She turns to leave and Jimmy moves to get between her and the door.

"I believe you, Janet. But you've got to realize that Sergeant Robson will keep questioning you until he finds out what happened to Martin. Don't you care about that? Doesn't it mean something to you? Remember, that's why you came to me in the first place. You wanted me to find the truth about your brother's death."

She shakes herself, like a dog expelling water from its coat. "I don't care. I don't remember anything more."

"All right. You saw the man with the lisp just once, with Martin, in front of your house. Did they act as if they were friends?"

"I want to leave."

"Janet . . ." Jimmy moves away from the door.

"I thought you wanted to help me. Instead you're being horrible." She wrenches the door open to find Lucille standing outside in the passage. Janet immediately transforms herself from a bellicose, obdurate child into a laughing, bubbly adolescent, and without bothering to look at Jimmy or say anything further to him, she takes Lucille's arm and the two girls descend the stairs.

The confrontation with Janet depresses Jimmy. He does not understand why she has been so evasive about the man with the lisp, when surely she must understand there could be a direct link between this person and the death of her brother. He looks at his watch, remembers his appointment with Evelyn Chan, sees he is twenty minutes late and wonders if he should skip his visit. But if he doesn't show up, he knows Evelyn will not allow him to see her again, and so he dashes down the stairs and races along the streets to her townhouse.

Perhaps the exercise energizes him, for Jimmy is agreeably surprised by the vigour of his performance when he and Evelyn Chan retire to the dimly lit bedroom and sandalwood-scented bed. Afterwards she tells Jimmy that when he did not show up at the agreed time she assumed he had decided to discontinue his visits. "Julie tells me you have found a sweetheart," she murmurs.

"Julie talks nonsense," Jimmy replies.

"She's rich, Julie says." She leans on her elbow to look at him. "Are you in love with her?"

"Yes, but I don't want to be."

"I've never been in love," Evelyn says, trailing her fingertips along Jimmy's chest and stomach. "What's it like?"

"It affects your view of the world."

"Makes it rosier?"

"No. It multiplies the uncertainties."

"And you prefer certainties . . . like this?" She straddles Jimmy and unites their bodies. But, irked by her comment, Jimmy sits up, pushes Evelyn off and turns her onto her stomach. He shoves a pillow under her hips and enters her roughly.

"Oh, I liked that," she says a few minutes later. "Do you and your sweetheart do that?" Jimmy shakes his head.

"Julie thinks you'll probably marry her."

"Julie's dreaming." Jimmy decides it is time for him to leave, and as he puts on his clothes, he tells Evelyn Chan that while marriage with Janet might be desirable, the likelihood of it happening is nil.

"Oh, you never know," she says. "By the way, I saw your uncle the other day. He tells me he's staying in Vancouver for a while." When Jimmy informs her he doesn't care what his uncle does, so long as he does it far away from him, she laughs. "You two strike sparks off each other," she says as she leaves the bed and walks to a full-length mirror to look at herself. "It's because you're so much alike."

That Evelyn Chan should think his behaviour bears any resemblance to his uncle's astounds Jimmy, and after telling her that she must be losing her wits, he walks home to Union Street. There he finds Janet, Lucille and Annette at the dinner table. Lucille tells him that Janet is spending the night, and later when they adjourn to the small sitting room to talk and watch TV, Lucille and Janet flop down on Annette's precious Chinese carpet. Jimmy, who sits on the couch alongside Annette, hopes Janet will lean against his legs. Instead, she reclines on Annette as though it is the most natural thing in the world to do. It occurs to Jimmy that perhaps Janet sees in Annette the energetic, authoritarian parent she has never had, the mother who issues orders while lovingly directing her daughter on the road toward a happy and secure future. Annette reinforces this notion by ordering Lucille to fetch a hair brush, which she vigorously uses on Janet's thick, glistening hair, while emphatically announcing that girls must always look their best, inside and out.

"Mother . . ." Jimmy attempts to intervene.

But Annette ignores him and sweeps on, punctuating her dogma with brisk movements of the brush. "Girls must always think of their hair and skin." She then delivers a lecture on the relationships between daily consumption of fruit and vegetables, the orderly movement of the bowels, a clear, smooth complexion, and a glossy head of hair. It embarrasses Jimmy, but it apparently has little effect on Janet, who seems to be in a state of semi-hypnosis induced by the methodical movements of the brush across her scalp and the rhythm of flickering images on the TV screen. "There! That's better," Annette says. "You're even prettier than before." Janet does not speak, but turns to smile at Annette.

The idyllic little family gathering comes to an end promptly at nine-thirty when Annette turns off the TV, explaining to Janet that they go to bed early because they are up at five-thirty each morning to shop at the wholesale market. Later, as Jimmy is lying in bed, listening to the murmur of voices in the adjacent bedroom, he thinks of Janet removing her clothes and getting into bed with Lucille. This image resurrects that part of Jimmy's body which has so recently been reduced to quiescence in Evelyn Chan's bed, but he soon drifts off into a dreamless sleep. He awakens to scents and sounds that tell him Annette is downstairs waiting for him. Before descending the stairs, he cautiously opens the door to Lucille's room and peeps in to see two duvet-covered bodies curled against each other like snoozing cats.

Annette and Jimmy seldom talk during their early morning ritual. Today, as Jimmy watches people coming and going in the market and looks at the massive produce trailers waiting to disgorge their contents, it occurs to him drug runners have no need to create new, exotic methods for transporting their wares across borders when an everyday transport and distribution system like this one is available for their use at almost any location around the world. Jimmy begins to look through new eyes at the familiar crates and boxes in the market. Is it possible while in transit they have nestled up against containers of white powder? He realizes the discovery of cocaine in Martin's apartment has thrust him into an alien world. Besides his lack of knowledge about the drug world, Jimmy knows he is prone to indulge in endless speculation on subjects of which he is ignorant.

Jimmy waits, sipping coffee, while Annette completes her purchases. Afterwards, they load them into the car and take them to the store before returning home, where they join Lucille and Janet for breakfast. The girls are still wearing their flower-patterned flannelette nightgowns, and Jimmy finds them both heart-achingly beautiful. Janet tells Annette she would like to accompany her to the market one morning, a request which pleases Annette, although she scoffs and says, "It's no big deal. Just a lot of boxes and cartons filled with fruit and vegetables. But if you want to come along one morning, it's fine with me."

"Don't bother, Janet " Lucille comments. "It's one huge bore!" After providing this assessment, Lucille goes upstairs to get dressed, and Janet follows.

When the girls are gone, Annette makes a rare gesture; she reaches across the table and places her hand on top of Jimmy's. "That's a lovely girl, Jimmy. She's just right for you."

"Mother . . ." Jimmy stops, knowing anything he says will be a waste of breath.

"She's is a good worker too. I can tell from watching her in the store. And I know she'll have strong, healthy babies. She's eaten fresh fruit and vegetables all her life."

Jimmy looks at his mother, pats the hand which covers his and thinks of all the people around the world like her who are governed by implacable, indestructible dreams of love and romance. "Mother . . . Mother . . ." Jimmy whispers.

And so they sit there, mother and son, motionless, he waiting for events to unfold, she for the impossible to come true.

8

Jimmy vividly remembers this particular morning in his life: he sees himself seated at his desk, going through a client's file, when he hears Annette walk along the passage to the bathroom. (He would recognize her quick, decisive step anywhere.) She returns, descends the stairs, and minutes pass before Jimmy hears her calling. He walks to the head of the stairs and looks down at her.

"She's gone!" Annette calls up. "She's gone!"

Odd though it now seems, Jimmy does not immediately grasp what Annette is saying, and when he realizes his mother is referring to Janet, he races down the stairs and into the store where he does all the ridiculous things people do when they lose something they value.

"What happened, Mother? Did Janet tell you she was leaving?"

Annette shakes her head. "No. I asked her to look after the store for a few minutes while I went to the toilet. Where could she have gone? Could she have run over to Julie and Bill's? Oh dear, I didn't think . . . maybe she needed something . . . you know . . . oh dear, I should have asked Lucille where she keeps hers before she left. Quick, go and see."

By now Jimmy realizes running wildly around is a waste of time. Nevertheless, he hurries through the typically dense Chinatown traffic to Bill Wong's store, where Julie is contentedly leaning against the cash register. He calls, "Is Janet here?"

But before Julie finishes saying "No, why do you want to know?" Jimmy is already tearing back across the street, where Annette tells him to check at the corner drugstore and then at Harry Lee's. He does this, then brings things to a halt and tells Annette he is going upstairs to telephone Sergeant Robson. After being told Robson is not available, he leaves an urgent request to return his call, then hunches into his chair and tries to figure out what might have happened to Janet.

From downstairs, Jimmy can hear Annette negotiating a sale with Mrs. Chang, a regular customer, who either does not know she is deaf, or knows, but refuses to wear a hearing aid.

"Lovely spinach today, Mrs. Chang," shrieks Annette.

"Yes, much better," hollers Mrs. Chang.

"You want some?" Annette yells, and Jimmy assumes she is now holding a bundle of spinach aloft. "Four bunches should be enough," she shrieks on, informing Mrs. Chang that spinach will add strength and vitality to Mr. and Mrs. Chang's marital activities.

Annette must have performed some descriptive callisthenics, because Mrs. Chang screeches, "Mr. Chang don't need no more strengthening. He's over my side of the bed most every night." (Jimmy tries to imagine it, Mr. Chang being a quiet, respectable member of the Chinese community, a butcher by trade and an Episcopalian by creed.)

Jimmy can hear the two women laughing and slapping each others' backs and he comes close to disliking his mother for her callousness in carrying on a salacious conversation during a time of crisis in his life. Of course he knows that Annette must continue to deal as usual with her customers, just as he is aware that Mrs. Chang, who has put in close to thirty years of unremitting labour in her husband's butcher shop and borne and raised seven children in her spare time, feels an obligation every time she enters the store to remind Annette (poor widow) that she is missing the better part of life. But Mrs. Chang's innuendoes do not bother Annette. Her objective is to get rid of the spinach. "Let me know if your bed collapses," Annette yells as Mrs. Chang departs with the spinach.

It occurs to Jimmy that perhaps his mother had unwittingly said something that offended Janet, thus causing her to leave at the first opportunity. He goes down to the store and puts the question to Annette, who shakes her head and says, "We talked about general things, like getting married and having your own home."

"Mother . . ." Jimmy groans. "Janet already has a home."

"Young women need to get used to the idea of running a household. Let me tell you, it's not easy for some of them. They're not all like Julie. Anyway, it was no big deal."

Now Jimmy is convinced that Janet has fled because she was frightened by the plans his mother was concocting for her and Jimmy. "I'm going upstairs to call Robson again," he says, and escapes.

Jimmy moons around in his office for a while, interrupted only by Julie, who crosses the street to supply him with a couple of reasons for Janet's disappearance, which turn out to be no help whatsoever. Before leaving Julie gives Jimmy a hug and kiss as always, tells him not to worry and hurries back to her store.

After Julie's departure, Jimmy finds he cannot remain in the office. As each minute passes the room becomes more oppressive. Finally he leaves, telling Annette he is going to Harry Lee's and asking her to direct Robson to the cafe should he telephone or show up at the store. In the cafe, Harry Lee wants to know where Janet is.

"She's busy," Jimmy snaps. "I'll have a bowl of soup."

Harry Lee obligingly fetches the soup and lingers at the table to gossip, even though Jimmy gestures dismissal. But Harry is determined to tell the story of how he hunted for years before he found a woman who would marry him, and what he has had to do over the years to keep her happy. As Harry brings his saga to a close, the cafe door swings open and Robson enters, his large presence seeming to reduce the room to a third its actual size. He strides to Jimmy's table and sits.

"You want soup?" Harry asks.

"For chrissake no! I don't want soup. Hey, can you make a decent hamburger?" Robson asks.

"Harry's a fine cook," Jimmy sourly answers. "He can prepare anything. Just tell him what you want."

Robson now explains how to prepare his hamburger: medium rare, onions gently sauteed, lettuce fresh, tomatoes sliced very thin. "And go easy on the mayo, okay?" Robson concludes his instructions, waves Harry away and turns to Jimmy. "Listen, Mr. Sung. When I got your telephone message I called the MacDougail house. Janet is there, so you can quit your worrying."

"You expect me to believe Janet walked away from the store and went home?"

"I don't care what you believe. Kindly remember the girl's a minor and Mrs. MacDougail is her guardian. The TV cameras and reporters left and Mrs. MacDougail wanted her granddaughter back home. Simple explanation."

"So somebody came and got Janet?"

Robson shrugs. "Maybe. And there's nothing you can do about it, Mr. Sung."

"Janet's my client."

"That isn't the impression I got from the old lady. And I heard something else, too. It seems Beasley saw you sitting with Janet on the stairs the other evening. Mrs. MacDougail more or less told me she doesn't want Janet mixing with any oriental types, though that's not what she called you."

"That old bitch!" The epithet explodes from Jimmy, and once it is out he is ashamed of having uttered it.

Robson smiles. "Sure, the world's jam-packed with bitches, and plenty of bastards too. You didn't know that?"

"I'm a Canadian, Sergeant Robson. My family has been in this country since before the turn of the century, which is probably more than be said of yours."

"Of course you're a Canadian, Mr. Sung. But do you suppose Mrs. MacDougail gives a shit about that?" Harry Lee brings a hamburger to the table and watches as Robson first critically eyes it, then takes an enormous bite, reflectively chews, swallows and nods his head. "Hm! Not bad . . . not bad at all." He takes another huge bite.

Harry Lee smiles satisfaction. "See? Jimmy told you I was a good cook, eh?"

"Yeah, sure. Bring some coffee, will you?" Robson calls as Harry, radiating delight, returns to his grill and soup pots.

"My eight-year-old daughter has discovered cooking," Robson comments after swallowing the remainder of the hamburger, "and she expects me to eat whatever she fixes. I say it's great stuff. She's so darn sweet I can't bring myself to tell her she'll probably finish off my digestive system for good. It's funny how love affects some guys. I mean, look at you. You're a wreck."

"I'm not." Jimmy attempts assertiveness, and fails.

"Yes you are," Robson says derisively. "Any objectivity you may once have had about this case is now kaput. All you can think about is that girl. This being so, Mr. Sung, you'd better take yourself out of this investigation. I can tell you from experience, once you lose your objectivity you're finished." Harry comes with the coffee, which Robson noisily slurps. "And here's another reason you should butt out: you're an itty-bitty minnow swimming around in deep waters, and unless you stay where you belong, Mr. Sung, you're going to run into some ferocious sharks, and that'll be the end of you."

Jimmy tries to defend himself. "I'll be okay, Sergeant. I'm smarter than you think."

"Hm! Let me tell you something about the MacDougails, Mr. Sung. They've been operating in the States for a long time, since the start of the American Civil War. They set themselves up as merchants, buying cotton in the south and selling it in the north, then buying guns in the north to sell in the south. They made themselves a helluva lot of money out of that operation. Then they branched out and began making and selling patent medicines to all the folks in North America with aches and pains—and there was no shortage of those. Ever heard of laudanum, Mr. Sung? It's made from opium that's mixed up with a bunch of other stuff. Laudanum was real popular in the nineteenth century, except nobody knew they were taking laudanum every time they took a slug of a

MacDougail elixir. And the MacDougails had no trouble getting all the opium they needed. Maybe they even did business with some of your ancestors, Mr. Sung. Anyway, the family continued to make real big money. Nowadays they're into almost every profitable economic activity in North America. And they're respectable, real respectable. Don't ever forget that, Mr. Sung. They stay away from booze, gambling, and prostitution and leave all that sort of stuff to the mobs. Want to know where I got all this info, Mr. Sung? From the FBI. And according to the FBI, the MacDougails have no objection to making a few billion bucks on the side supplying narcotic dealers with the purest of pure heroin and cocaine, although the FBI has never been able to make a case against them that'll stick. The FBI has even thrown out hints that the MacDougails are untouchable. So there you have it, Mr. Sung, all laid out for you, nice and handy."

"So where does Martin MacDougail fit into all this?" Jimmy asks.

"I have no idea. But what I do know is the MacDougails are very concerned about keeping their noses clean. They don't want someone like you—or me—poking around in their affairs. See what I mean?"

"Not exactly."

Robson smiles at Jimmy. "Here's something else you ought to think about, Mr. Sung. The MacDougails are big philanthropists too. I'm told someone in the family even has a hospital named after him, in Maine or some fucking place like that. And listen to this, Mr. Sung—and this is a matter of public record—they sponsor an organization devoted to facilitating entry of orphan children into North America for adoption."

"Wait a minute . . ."

"And I've left out a lot of things they do, Mr. Sung, like the fact that one of their companies can supply you with a new organ for your body. Hey, whatever you might need—a heart, kidney, liver, maybe even a new dork—though they don't necessarily tell you anything about their source of supply. Want to know anything else, Mr. Sung?"

"I want to know why you're telling me all this."

"It should be obvious. Should be *fucking* obvious. It's a picture you don't belong in. Just get out!" Robson pushes back his chair and stands.

"So what about the murder of Betty Nelson? And what about Martin MacDougail? Are you going to forget those deaths? Is that what you're telling me?"

"Don't you worry, Mr. Sung, I won't forget anything. I'm just telling *you* to forget it. It's good advice, and I suggest you follow it." Robson turns and goes to the cash register where Harry Lee gives him a receipt marked paid. Robson tears it up, puts a ten-dollar bill on the cash register and walks out. Harry Lee shakes his head, then comes across to Jimmy's table.

"What do you make of that guy, Jimmy?"

"I don't make anything of him," Jimmy says as he stands and puts a two-dollar bill on the table.

"Put that away. He paid for your soup."

"I don't want him to pay for anything I eat. Take it." Jimmy exits, leaving behind a thoroughly bewildered Harry Lee.

When Jimmy gets back to the store Lucille immediately commands him to mount a raid to rescue Janet. "Stay out of it," orders Jimmy, as he passes her and climbs the stairs to his office, where he sits and morosely eyes the wall. Part of him acknowledges the validity of what Robson has said. He is aware he has no business involving himself any further in the affairs of the MacDougails. But, overriding anything Robson might say to convince him to drop his investigation, is Jimmy's overwhelming sense of loss at the thought of never seeing Janet again. This produces an unbearable feeling of emptiness in him, as though somebody close has died and everything of value cruelly squeezed from his life. Jimmy goes over what Robson has told him about the MacDougails, including the implied warnings, but because his emotionally-charged state of mind prevents him from thinking rationally, he dismisses Robson's advice, preferring the comfort of constructing a dream in which he rescues Janet and saves her from a gang of evil relatives. And, though he understands quite well Janet may not wish to be rescued, still he continues to embroider his dream because it dulls the ache inside him. He even goes to bed that night with the intention of enhancing the dream by adding scenes involving acrobatic sex and avowals of mutual love between him and Janet. Instead, he dreams that Harry Lee is showing him how to make hamburgers. Harry stands before an enormous grill on which dozens of hamburgers splatter and fizzle. "This is how you do it, Jimmy" Harry says, as Emily appears, carrying their small daughter Emerald. "Press them down real good, Jimmy," explains Harry, just as Emily hurls Emerald at Jimmy. He ducks and Emerald, who is wearing underpants with multitudinous frills, lands on the grill and begins sizzling. Harry brings up a spatula and flattens her while shouting, "This is the way you do it, Jimmy. You keep pressing and pressing and pressing." He then takes up the flattened Emerald, puts her into a bun, and hands it to Jimmy, while yelling "Eat! Eat! That's a perfect hamburger. The best you'll ever taste." Jimmy opens his mouth about to consume an Emerald burger when he is awakened by the rattle of his alarm.

"You don't look so good," Annette says to Jimmy when he walks into the kitchen. "Feeling sick? Are your bowels all right?"

"I had a nightmare, that's all."

As they are driving towards the market Annette suggests, "You should have a talk with Uncle Jimmy. He might know what to do about Janet."

For the first time in his life Jimmy is rude to Annette. "Bull shit, Mother! Uncle Jimmy knows bugger-all!"

Annette draws herself up and glares at Jimmy. "You're forgetting yourself," she says. "Forgetting who I am, who your uncle is." Jimmy mumbles an apology, though he tells himself it is only for Annette. "Your uncle knows lots of important people, and he's good at handling problems."

There the conversation ends. Annette conducts her business at the market and they return home to find Lucille in foul humour because she will not be spending the weekend with

Janet. She snarls at Jimmy, snaps at Annette, then informs them both she won't be attending classes today and may choose never return to school. She stomps up to her room, where she sulks until Annette collects her and takes her to the store. Jimmy goes to his office, where he accomplishes nothing. Later in the morning, when the mail arrives, among the letters he sees a plain white envelope. Inside it he finds a cheque signed by Margaret MacDougail for five thousand dollars, the largest single amount of money his rat-tail business has earned since he started it. He is still staring at the cheque when Lucille enters with a doughnut and a cup of coffee to effect a reconciliation. She leans on his shoulder and eats the doughnut while Jimmy drinks the coffee. The sounds of Lucille chewing reverberate in his left ear. "I telephoned Janet, but a man answered and told me she wasn't available. Jimmy, you must go to the house and insist on seeing Janet. Maybe something awful has happened to her."

"Sergeant Robson said Janet left the store and went home of her own accord."

Lucille presses her face against his. Jimmy has never been able to resist an unhappy Lucille. She curls herself around him like a cat rubbing against its owner's ankles, and tries to persuade him to talk things over with Uncle Jimmy. When Jimmy temporizes, she reacts with anger.

"You're behaving like a fool!" she screams. "If you refuse to talk to Uncle Jimmy about this, I'll never forgive you. Besides, it's you I'm thinking of, Jimmy. I feel Janet is just the right person for you. I feel it right here." She presses her hand against her blouse.

"In your blouse?" Jimmy teases.

"No!" she flares. "In my heart. And anyway, all I'm asking is that you talk things over with Uncle Jimmy." She hugs Jimmy and rubs her face against his. "Please."

"Has Mother been talking to Uncle?"

"He telephoned her. You know how he calls her in the mornings."

Eventually Jimmy agrees to see Uncle Jimmy, not because

Ernest Langford

he thinks his uncle can actually help, but only to appease
Lucille. At once, Lucille informs him Uncle Jimmy has invited
him for lunch at an exclusive downtown club.

So, at one o'clock, Jimmy finds himself standing at the
door of the club. He explains to someone guarding the entrance
why he is there, waits while his statement is confirmed, and
then is escorted to the table where his uncle sits.

"Nephew," Uncle Jimmy begins as soon as Jimmy is
seated, "I hear you've misplaced someone. Well, I'm not too
surprised."

The already overwrought Jimmy, angered by the implied
insult, retaliates. "If that's the advice you have to offer, there's
no point in me staying." He begins to stand.

"Sit down!" Uncle Jimmy orders. "You did lose the young
lady, didn't you?"

"I don't know what actually happened. I wasn't in the
store when she left." Jimmy takes out and shows his uncle the
envelope he received that morning in the mail.

Uncle Jimmy opens the envelope and sniffs. "I had no idea
your services were so high-priced. Remind me not to employ
you."

"I'll go out of my way to do just that."

Uncle Jimmy briefly smiles. "Don't imitate my bad habits,
Nephew," he remarks as he returns the envelope together with
a folded copy of the *Vancouver Province*. "Did you see this report
in the morning newspaper?" he asks, pointing to the headlines
on the front page.

Jimmy reads the report.

FORMER CITY SOCIALITE FOUND DEAD IN FARMHOUSE

The body of a man identified as that of William F. MacDougail
was found yesterday by three children in a deserted house on
the Fraser river flats in Burnaby. The children, who were
looking for their lost puppy, entered the house thinking their
dog might be there.

A Burnaby RCMP spokesperson stated that MacDougail

128

appeared to have been dead for some days. Cause of death has not yet been determined.

Fifteen years ago, MacDougail was part of a group of socially prominent people questioned by Vancouver City Police and the RCMP in connection with the importation of illegal substances into Canada. Subsequently MacDougail dropped from the social scene and became a recluse.

Another member of the MacDougail family interviewed by the police was killed a few days later in a boating accident when their luxurious yacht the *Elizabeth* exploded and burned in Burrard Inlet. Marine experts agreed the accident was caused by pockets of gas that had collected in the bilge and fuel tanks.

The Vancouver MacDougail family is a branch of the giant US MacDougail financial and industrial empire.

Jimmy carefully lays the newspaper on the white-clothed table and looks across at his uncle. "What am I expected to conclude from reading this?" he asks.

"I like to think, Nephew, that you possess a modicum of intelligence," Uncle Jimmy begins. "But I want you to keep in mind that I am someone who has had considerable experience in the world, a person capable of judging when caution should govern one's conduct."

"I'm not sure I understand what you're getting at, Uncle. But what I know for sure is that one day a young woman appeared in my office and asked me to look into her brother's death. At the time I had no idea who the girl was, but I agreed to help her. The fact that her brother is apparently turning out to be a cocaine dealer has nothing to do with me. Nor is the fact that an uncle is found dead, or that a former girlfriend of her brother is murdered. None of that is my responsibility. But the fact that Janet MacDougail was in Mother's store when she vanished is my responsibility. And while it might be true I regard Janet MacDougail with some affection, it's beside the point."

"The girl is safe."

"Who put you up to this meeting anyway?" Jimmy leans

over the table. "Did that old bitch tell you to try to stop me from seeing Janet? Well, let me tell you something, Uncle. From now on, even if you are a member of my family, I insist you stop giving me orders and expecting me to jump every time you open your mouth."

Uncle Jimmy slowly pushes back his chair and gets to his feet. Jimmy sees that his uncle is shaking, although he cannot determine whether from rage or shock. "You are behaving foolishly," Uncle Jimmy says, his voice hardly more than a whisper. "Get away from me . . . get away."

Seething with anger, Jimmy leaves the building, but once in the street he regains a degree of objectivity and recognizes he should have behaved more politely and have pretended to listen to his uncle, even though whatever Uncle Jimmy might have to say was probably not going to be of any use to him.

Jimmy knows he cannot return to the office. His uncle will have already telephoned Annette with a report of his behaviour and the minute he steps into the door a bombardment of questions will be certain to greet him. So he drifts aimlessly around the streets, not knowing what to do next. At every intersection he half expects to see Janet coming along the street to meet him at the corner. More than anything in the world, Jimmy wants Janet to be physically present and walking beside him, but since she cannot be there, he imagines her as she goes about her daily rituals—getting up in the morning, removing and putting on clothes, bathing and drying her pellucid skin, eating meals, walking down the street. Above all else, Jimmy imagines himself touching and exploring Janet's body. But what if she does not ever return his love, Jimmy asks himself. What then? Surely his love can suffice for both. Sexual relations between a man and a woman need not necessarily involve love—look at him and Evelyn Chan, they come together in order to satisfy a physical need each has. While Jimmy concedes that sexual satisfaction can be enhanced by love, it need not be present. But Jimmy would always treat Janet with great tenderness, he knows that. His experience with Evelyn Chan had shown him how to satisfy a woman's sexual needs and he swears to himself he would approach Janet as a devotee at a shrine.

The afternoon passes as Jimmy walks south on Granville Street. As evening settles on the city, and lights appear in houses Jimmy finds himself staring across the boulevard at Janet's house. He crosses, walks past the driveway, goes to the end of the street, turns the corner and walks on until he comes to the laneway which passes behind the row of houses. For the first time since hurrying off to his disastrous meeting with his uncle, Jimmy consults his watch and finds the time to be almost ten o'clock. Because he cannot immediately decide what action he should take, he walks the full length of the block and arrives back at the alley. But now he moves with care, counting the rooftops as he passes garage entries until he reaches the high fence behind the MacDougail house.

There Jimmy stands, listening to the sound of his own breathing and remembering an acquaintance at university once telling him of an experience while camping beside a lake in northern BC. At night, the guy said with awe in his voice, the stillness became so absolute he could hear water trickling down the mountain on the other side of the six-kilometre-wide lake. It was as though, he said, one were listening to the sound of infinity, the all-encompassing voice of the universe. At the time, Jimmy wondered if his acquaintance had really wanted to say 'the voice of God', but had been too embarrassed to utter the words. Now, leaning against the fence and listening to the far-off hum of traffic on Granville, Jimmy wonders if what his friend was trying to say was that silence, or more precisely, that which we call silence, is actually filled with sounds which we may, or may not, choose to hear.

But why, Jimmy asks himself, am I wasting time now thinking about what someone told me years ago, when I should be taking decisive action to rescue Janet? He recalls a dream that recurred many times during his school years: Jimmy is trying to cross a river by jumping from rock to rock, and as he hops, the river widens and rises, threatening to engulf him as he frantically tries to spring forward. He thinks now the dream was a manifestation of his anxiety, but at the time he was too preoccupied with his studies to conceive of the possibility his subconscious mind was telling him something about himself that required his attention. It appears to Jimmy, as he stands alone in the darkness, that his entire being during his school years—when he was a whiz kid—had been a void, which he tried to fill with knowledge from books and teachers, indiscriminately chewing up information at one end and spewing it out at the other in the form of term papers, essays and exam answers. He had likened himself then to a computer, which can only give back what somebody else has put in; in those days he thought of himself as a person who could not function unless somebody switched him on.

Jimmy thinks, am I capable of more now? Because I am older (and wiser?) do I stand a better chance of being able to grasp directly the essence of things without the aid of logical reasoning? But even supposing I can do this, what if I don't know how or where to apply what I perceive? What then? What if I am not able to take decisive action based on my perceptions? Might I end up like Hamlet, unable to take any action because he had lost himself in an examination of the reasons for taking it? Look at me now. At the very moment I should be devising a way to rescue Janet, here I am, leaning against a fence in a laneway, doodling and dithering over my adolescent years in the academic wilderness. So enough of this mooning about. I say no more procrastination. I must take action! I will take action! Now!

Jimmy hooks his hands over the fence and pulls himself up to lie along the top of it, while at the same time trying to see what lies below and to distinguish the outline of the house, with its mansard roof and heavily curtained windows. He swings around, drops down into a bed of soft garden soil and makes his away toward the house along a brick path, almost walking into the deep end of an empty swimming pool. He knows about the side door through which Martin used to visit Janet, and he follows the path to the left and comes to a wall where he smells oil and car polish. Back he goes, past the pool, walking carefully, to the other side of the house where the path curves inward to end at a door.

There he stands, feeling neither courageous nor rash, licking his lips and rubbing his nose. He thinks about the time in grade two that he got into a fight with another boy; even now, he can see the boy advancing toward him, fists clenched. Jimmy recalls he began crying and wet his pants before whirling his arms around windmill fashion and knocking off the boy's glasses, which another boy immediately stepped on and smashed.

Now Jimmy shivers with anticipation, fervently praying the door will be locked. When the handle turns and the door opens, Jimmy actually thinks of himself as one of the world's unluckiest people. He finds himself in a dark passage and begins to walk forward. So preoccupied is he with being quiet that he slams into an inside door which rattles as he hits it. This frightens him so much he bolts outside, but, since lights do not flash nor people rush out to apprehend him, he creeps back to the inner door and turns the handle. When it opens, he finds himself looking into a high-ceilinged, shelf-lined storeroom. The shelves are filled with all manner of canned, bottled and packaged food and other household items, and Jimmy thinks the inhabitants must have a siege mentality. He has an impulse to giggle and slaps his cheeks to quell the urge. He moves to the storeroom door and presses his ear against it, while remembering the steely-nerved private eyes he has seen on TV, who enter buildings and rooms without being seen and lead charmed lives as bullets and knives flow around them like light rays from distant stars bending around the sun.

The door opens onto a large, brightly lit but deserted kitchen. Afterwards, Jimmy will vaguely recall seeing at least two stoves, a massive refrigerator and many copper pots hanging from the ceiling, but at the time he is totally focused on the stairway. Carpet covers the stairs, for which Jimmy is grateful. He goes up them, step by step, and reaches a passage which ends at a door Jimmy feels certain will take him into the MacDougail-occupied section of the house. There are five doors which open into the passage, four on the sides and one at the end of the hall; bars of light at floor level shine through three of the doors. Jimmy moves along the passageway, opens the door at the end, and slides through. Now the carpet is thickly piled and Jimmy sees to his right the staircase where he had sat with Janet, leading down into the central hall. The passage is wide and the room doors are conveniently ajar. To his left is a very large bedroom with ornate mahogany furniture. There is a bathroom further down the hall, what looks like a guest room, and two more bedrooms; one stripped down (this room must once have been Martin's) and the other Jimmy knows is Janet's because of her scent lingering in the air.

Jimmy enters the room, closes the door and looks around. He fixes on a series of photographs arranged on top of a chest of drawers. There is Janet as a baby, being cradled in a woman's arms (her mother?) and several others showing her at different ages, either in or beside the swimming pool. In one, she looks about two or three years old and is being held over the pool by a smiling man, whose face suggests he is her father. In another, Janet is poised on the diving board, arms stretched above her head, and although Jimmy resists the idea, he is reminded of the naked girl in the picture hanging in the house where Betty Nelson lay dead. The rest of the pictures are school portraits. Now Jimmy begins to open drawers in the two dressers, hoping the contents will reveal something. Inside the first are folded tee shirts, in another a jumble of underclothes and stockings. He fights a powerful urge to lift these garments to his face, not to satisfy any sexual impulse, but simply because they have touched Janet's body.

Finally he leaves the room, and as he walks along the passage, hears voices in the central hall. He creeps to the stairway, moves down to the landing and peers into the hall below. There he sees a tall man on the weather side of middle age speaking to somebody standing outside on the doorstep. The timbre of the man's voice suggests he is an individual well bolstered by strata upon strata of impregnable stocks, bonds, and trust funds. "Yes, yes, I know . . . Quite right . . . It's very upsetting." He pauses while the person in the darkness outside speaks, and although Jimmy cannot distinguish what words are being said, the sibilant sounds forcibly remind Jimmy of someone he knows. "I know . . . two sons, then the grandson . . . yes . . . I don't know . . . no explanation . . . none . . . oh really . . . that's quite a coincidence . . . yes, I'm sure it will all work out . . . I must get back to Margaret . . . yes, a difficult time for her . . . I'm returning to Los Angeles on the nine-thirty flight . . . I'll tell her . . . good night." As the door closes, Jimmy retreats into the darkness and hears the man walk across the hall. Jimmy thinks if he acts quickly enough he may be able to get out of the house and around to the front of the property in time to identify the person outside. He debates leaving by the main entrance, but instead turns and hurries up the stairs where he comes face-to-face with Beasley.

"Hey! You!" Beasley exclaims and grabs at Jimmy, who first jumps back, then literally hurls himself beneath Beasley's clutching hands, forcing him to stumble forward onto his knees. Jimmy has no memory of leaving the house. All he remembers is running along Granville Street, waving down a cab, getting into it, giving the driver the address of his office, then collapsing in the back seat, too spent to consider his next move.

Of course Jimmy clearly understands what he must do, and he does it as soon as he reaches his office. He telephones the airport and has no trouble locating the airline with a nine-thirty flight to Los Angeles the next morning. "I'm sorry, sir," the ticket agent at the other end of the line says. "All seats are booked."

"It's important for me to be on that flight!"

"Sorry," the agent says. "The best I can do is put you on standby."

"I *must* be on that flight." Jimmy repeats.

"We have other departures to Los Angeles during the day." The agent's voice has ceased to be pert and cheerful and is now distant and chilly.

"I don't want to go on a later flight. Put me on standby." Jimmy tries wheedling and excessive explanation. "Look, I'm involved in a murder investigation," he begins, while thinking the agent is labelling him a flake, or even insane, but what else can he do? "There's a man on that plane I must watch. I need to find out where he's going. I'll give you the telephone number of the police officer I'm working with. Call him and he'll verify what I'm telling you." Jimmy rattles off Robson's name and telephone number, knowing the agent won't call, and even if she did her chances of contacting Robson would be infinitesimal.

But Jimmy's pitch must be having some effect because she

says, "I'll see what I can do, but for the moment I can't guarantee you a seat."

"Do your best," Jimmy pleads and offers profuse thanks, hoping thereby to have his name moved from the bottom of the standby list to the top. Jimmy also supplies her with his credit card number, crossing his fingers that by the time the charge clears he will have sufficient money to pay for the ticket and for any unforeseeable holdovers in Los Angeles. Jimmy metaphorically kicks himself for not having deposited Mrs. Mac-Dougail's check. He takes it out, writes his name and account number on the back, puts it inside a deposit envelope and walks down the street to the bank, where he slips the envelope into the night deposit slot. At home, he finds Annette stirring a big pot of soup stock on the stove. Jimmy realizes that the image of his mother standing at the stove preparing meals is the foundation on which he has erected the flimsy structure he calls his life. What's more, the only reason he has been able to get by with such a shaky edifice is because its foundation is so completely reliable. Jimmy tastes the stock and, as always, twigs Annette. "Not enough salt," he says.

Annette snatches the spoon from Jimmy to sip the brown liquid. "What d'you mean, not enough? There's plenty. Just the right amount. Anyway, you're salty enough as it is."

"Don't blame me for that, Mother. Whatever I am, came from you."

"I wouldn't be too sure of that." She turns off the gas and puts the lid on the big pot. "Where've you been?"

"Business."

"Why did you pick a fight with Uncle Jimmy? He's sure upset."

"I let him know exactly where I stand, that's all."

"It's not right, Jimmy. He's your . . . close relative."

"Maybe. But I'm not going to allow him to order me around any more."

"He doesn't mean to. It's just his way. He's fond of you, Jimmy."

"He has a strange way of showing it."

"He's always been like that. He doesn't know how to show affection." She sighs. "I wish you hadn't said those things to him." Annette is so upset she wrings her hands, something Jimmy had read about people doing but had never actually seen anyone do before. He puts an arm around her shoulders to comfort her.

"Mother, if you want me to apologize, I'll swallow my pride and do it. Okay?"

"You don't understand. Uncle Jimmy's helped me a lot. He's done a lot for you too."

"What! What's he ever done for me?"

"He helped pay your university tuition. He spoke to people and helped you get your private investigator's licence. We don't pay rent."

"I'll pay back every cent he spent on me. To hell with him. *I'll* pay the rent. I'll do everything for myself, and for you. Then maybe he'll leave us alone." Jimmy is so angry he can hardly articulate the words.

"No." Annette brushes a hand across her face, and Jimmy is appalled to see she is crying. He reaches out to hold her. During his entire life this has never happened and he finds it unbearable; Annette's strength has always been his security blanket.

"Mother . . . Mother . . . don't . . . . If you want, I'll go down on my knees and tell him I'm sorry."

"No, it doesn't matter. It's . . . something else . . . . Anyway, you're home now."

"I'll probably fly to Los Angeles tomorrow morning."

"Los Angeles! Why?"

"I think Janet's there. I'm going to get her."

"No. You don't know where she is. Why're you carrying on like this, Jimmy? I'm going to call your uncle." Annette breaks away and goes to the telephone. Jimmy follows and puts a hand over the dial.

"Mother, I know exactly what I am doing," he says. "Don't drag him into this."

"He's got a right."

"He has no right. None. I'm taking my hand off the phone, and it'll be up to you to decide if you're going to call him. But I'm warning you, Mother, if you do, you'll see me walk out of this house."

Jimmy removes his hand from the phone and looks at Annette's face as a profound struggle goes on within her. Her limbs tremble and her throat convulses as she fights the hand which reaches out to raise the telephone receiver. Then the tremors cease. She breathes deeply before saying, "You'll need money."

"I probably have enough—but I'd appreciate a loan of five hundred dollars for backup. I'll pay you back."

"It doesn't matter." Annette goes to a small cabinet, uses a minute key to unlock one of its drawers, removes the drawer, and from behind it takes out a brown envelope stuffed with rubber-banded packets of US twenty-, fifty- and hundred-dollar bills. Jimmy has long known of Annette's secret cache and has urged her to bank it. She has never counted the money in Jimmy's presence, but by merely looking at the bulk, he has guessed there must be several thousand dollars in the envelope. The only explanation Jimmy has been able to think of for Annette keeping such a large amount of cash in the house is that she fears a disaster might assail her one day and destroy the familiar supports in her life. In such an emergency she could immediately utilize her hidden package. She takes out some bills and hands them to Jimmy. "Here." Jimmy counts the bills and protests he does not need two thousand dollars. But Annette insists—perhaps for her, this is an emergency—and eventually he accepts it. "How do you know Janet's in Los Angeles?" she asks.

"I overheard two men talking."

"Who? Where?"

"There's no need for you to know. Better not to. Besides, Janet has relatives there."

"I wish you wouldn't do this, Jimmy. It's not worth it."

"I'll be fine." He puts his arm around Annette and draws her close to him, aware she is frightened. He can feel her trembling, and at the same time is surprised to feel her body's youthful firmness. Jimmy has never wanted to think of his mother as a woman who could become emotionally and physically involved with men, yet he knows she is not much older than Evelyn Chan, who thoroughly enjoys her sexual activities. (Did other people have problems thinking of their parents' sexual lives, especially their mother's? Or is he just ultra-squeamish? Jimmy will never be sure.) Jimmy supposes he is being stupid, but he has never been able to imagine Annette embracing the man who fathered him. He cannot imagine her being other than in a state of guarded readiness, as she is now, watchful, prepared to defend herself and her children. Jimmy leans over and presses his lips against her head. Has he ever fully appreciated the degree of his attachment to his mother? His love for her has been casual, an almost amused acceptance of her foibles, a tolerance of a person set in her ways. Although there have been moments when his mother's idiosyncrasies embarrassed him, Jimmy recognizes it is those same characteristics which make her lovable; they are components of the barrier she has methodically built up over the years to deal with her customers and to defend her children against encroachments from a harsh, indifferent world.

"What time is your flight?" When Jimmy gives the departure time Annette tells him he need not accompany her to the wholesale market in the morning.

"I'll have plenty of time."

"What'll I tell Uncle Jimmy when he telephones?"

"Say I'm on my way to Pouce Coupé."

Jimmy goes to his room and lies on his bed to wonder whether he is conducting his life properly. He hears Annette climb the stairs and the sound of her bedroom door close. Is he being inconsiderate? Maybe he should go to her room and reassure her. He gets up and finds he is walking off a bush plane with pontoons at a lake near Pouce Coupé. "But I'm going to Los Angeles," he protests. "How do I get out of here?"

"You walk," a voice rattles in his ear, "you walk, walk,

walk." Jimmy wakes up to the sound of the alarm beneath his pillow.

Jimmy and Annette are eating breakfast after their trip to the market when Lucille joins them. She spies Jimmy's flight bag and wants to know where he is going. She wrinkles her nose when she learns the destination is the Peace River country, saying she can't understand why any woman would want to run away to such a place. Jimmy enlightens her. "It's a safe place to hide in."

"I don't see why you waste your time searching for run-away wives," Lucille says. "Women should never have to run away from their husbands anyway. They should be able to live wherever they please." On her way out of the kitchen she says, "Don't get lost in the bush." Jimmy notices Lucille seems to have forgotten Janet and regrets he has not done the same. He, unfortunately, remembers everything. Is his phenomenal memory all that is left of his former self as a whiz kid?

Jimmy and Annette do not speak during the drive to the airport, but as they approach the main entrance to the terminal, Annette mutters, "I don't blame you for doing this, Jimmy, but do be careful. I don't want anything to happen to you."

Jimmy takes her hand and squeezes it. "It won't. I'm an awful coward, and it's the cowards who survive in this world, not the heroes."

He hugs Annette, watches her drive away, then enters the cavernous building and joins the lineup at the ticket counter.

When Jimmy introduces himself, the ticket agent scans a list and proffers a mechanical smile. "Mr. Sung! You're in luck this morning, sir. We've had a cancellation." He prepares Jimmy's ticket, hands it to him with a boarding pass and immediately transfers his attention to the person behind Jimmy.

Once, during his university years, Jimmy had briefly worked in a fish-packing plant where his job was spiking and placing incoming salmon onto a conveyor belt. There the fish were beheaded, gutted, de-tailed and washed before being chopped up and put into cans. As Jimmy walks through the long terminal, strange as it may seem, he feels like a piece of salmon on its way to be canned and processed. He passes through the security checkpoint, wonders why he is rushing off to Los Angeles, tells himself he is doing the right thing, goes through US customs and immigration and enters the waiting room outside the boarding gate where he hopes to spot the man he has half-seen the previous night at the MacDougail's house.

When the boarding call comes and no one resembling the man has yet appeared, Jimmy waits, not knowing what to do. At what seems like the last moment, his man—it has to be— arrives in a lightweight tan suit and brown tasselled loafers. He smiles as he offers his boarding pass to the smiling woman standing at the gate, bids her a pleasant good morning—his deep, well-modulated voice confirming his identity—and walks down the enclosed ramp into the plane, followed by Jimmy. Inside the plane, the man stops in the first-class section and puts a monogrammed briefcase into the overhead luggage compartment. As Jimmy passes to reach the economy seats, the man turns and glances at him for a moment. Jimmy fears he has been recognized but tells himself that's impossible.

Now, you would think that Jimmy, secure in the knowledge that he is packed with his quarry as tightly as salmon in a can, could simply relax and take up something to read during the flight. But being preoccupied with identifying the man, he has forgotten to arm himself with something to ward off boredom during the interregnum between takeoff in Vancouver rain and landing in Los Angeles smog. So, Jimmy can either sit and twiddle his thumbs or use one to flip through a magazine generously provided free of charge by the airline and filled with information on how Jimmy might spend his mother's money.

From his position in an aisle seat Jimmy can look forward into the first-class section, and just before the flight attendant closes the curtain between the sections, he observes the deference with which she treats the tan-suited man. Jimmy glances at the middle-aged passenger seated beside him and thinks he must be a sales manager of an automobile company, because he is completely immersed in statistical charts of car sales laid out on his seat tray. Jimmy imagines the man is on his way to a sales convention, where his presentation will energize a automotive sales force to imbibe more alcohol than is good for them. He pictures the man living in suburban Coquitlam with a wife and two teenaged children, surrounded by everything Ikea can offer. The vision sends Jimmy soundly to sleep, and he awakens to the sound of a voice informing informs passengers the aircraft has just passed east of San Francisco. Jimmy sees the curtain move. His quarry appears and walks along the aisle. Jimmy quickly closes his eyes again, but is aware the man has hesitated beside him, both going and coming, something which puzzles Jimmy because he is positive the man has never seen him before and can have no idea who he is or why he is on the plane.

After a few minutes Jimmy cautiously opens his eyes and sees that the man has disappeared back into the first-class section. Jimmy's seatmate is packing reports and charts into a briefcase. "So that's that," he says, smiling at Jimmy. "On your way to Disneyland?"

"No," Jimmy says.

"Oh." The man sounds disappointed. "I expect at least twenty-five percent of the folks on this flight are going to Disneyland. Business, eh?"

"Law," Jimmy says.

The man nods. "Interesting work. I was fascinated by numbers as a kid, so I ended up in economics, statistical analysis, specializing in transportation. You know, the effect transportation systems have on cultures. Fascinating subject."

"Indeed." Jimmy wonders just how wrong he can be in his assessment of people. He feels the plane lurch and tilt forward as it commences its long descent towards Los Angeles.

"Oh sure," the man agrees. "Almost everything to do with migration patterns is of some interest. Take, for instance, bird migration. How do you suppose it originated?"

"I've no idea," Jimmy admits.

"Neither have I," the man says, "but I'd say it had something to do with availability of food. Where d'you think all

those geese and ducks nested during the great ice ages, eh?
There's nothing to eat on icecaps. Right? They either got out
or died. That means the original migration route wasn't from
the south to the north, but from north to south, and all due to
pressures of climatic changes and food shortages. Ah, pressure,
pressure, pressure. Migrations are all the same, friend, and it
doesn't matter whether it's insects, animals, fish, birds, or
humans, they produce clogged routes—and jammed freeways
too. I'll bet a buck when this plane touches down everyone
stands up and blocks the aisle. Maybe if the door opened when
the plane was still tearing along the runway at a hundred miles
an hour, they'd try to get off it, because that's how internal
pressure operates. I suppose if you look at a societal structure
as a functioning organism—and why not?—it would follow that
if you pack something in at one end, something's bound to come
out at the other end, unless internal blockage occurs. And that,
my friend, is when you get severe social problems, such as we
have now."

"Clogged arteries?"

"Sure, social infarction."

Jimmy makes suitable noises in response, but does not
want to get mixed up with another fanatical hobby-horser—
Annette and her dietary regime is enough for him. Besides, he
has to keep a close eye on his man; wasn't there an incident
once where some guy, after robbing a bank, put on a parachute,
jumped out of a passenger plane and vanished? So Jimmy
politely nods while his companion talks about food supplies
and mass migrations and their effect on transportation systems
and trading patterns. What the man says is interesting, but it
doesn't register with Jimmy who, after glimpsing multitudinous buildings as the plane banks in its approach to Los
Angeles, is preoccupied with figuring out a way to track his
quarry once he leaves his first-class seat.

"A word of advice, friend," the man beside him says, "don't
get up with the mob. Wait. Remember that migratory movements go forward in pulses. Have you ever seen films of animal
migrations? Fascinating. Not long ago I saw a film of gnu

migration in Africa. The animals need water, and the only place they can get it is a small pool packed with crocodiles. So what happens? The animals get pushed into the pool—by pressure—smack into the jaws of the crocs. And that's analogous to human migration." The man chuckles and looks out the tiny window. "Ah, home again," he says, as the wheels smacked against the runway.

People begin leaving their seats and opening luggage compartments. "I'm in the midst of formulating a theory explaining what happens when blockages occur in transportation systems. Mass claustrophobia results, which in turn stimulates mass hysteria, which produces mass destruction and death. Arguably the end result is mass suicide. This raises a very important question. No, don't move," he says, placing a hand on Jimmy's arm as he prepares to stand. "Which is—does the construction of arterial transportation systems ultimately contribute to the decline of a society? Quite a proposition, eh?" Jimmy nods, while trying to ease himself from beneath the man's restraining arm. "See? You're already infected. I am too, but experience has taught me how to fight off the disease. Actually what I feel like doing is crawling over the seats and fighting my way to the front of the plane in order to be first out the door. That's why I'm talking to you, it controls my impulse to leap from my seat. Odd, isn't it, how we use strangers, people we'll never see again, for therapeutic purposes? Once, when I grabbed the arm of the woman sitting beside me, she assumed I was trying to make a pass at her. Mistaken assumptions are often made by people in crowded places. They imagine threats that do not exist. Ah . . . I believe the door has been opened and within a few minutes we'll be free."

"I have to go," Jimmy mutters.

"Remember the old adage—more haste, less speed," the man says as Jimmy wrenches his arm away, stands and tries to look over bobbing heads and moving arms to see if his quarry has left the plane. He senses that his fellow passenger has moved to stand beside him and that his mouth is now adjacent to Jimmy's left ear. "The common assumption is that improved transportation systems facilitate cultural and industrial development, but in fact the reverse is true: the systems cause breaches in the cultural dams through which the waters of stability can rush out."

"I have to go," Jimmy whispers. "It's been very interesting, but . . ." He wriggles and squirms his way between the people in front, who protest by sternly glaring at him. Suddenly he finds himself free of the plane and running along a passage to a baggage collection point, where he abruptly halts, staring wildly around at the carousels, until he spots his quarry talking to a man wearing a chauffeur's uniform. Jimmy now grasps that he is faced with what could be an insurmountable problem, namely, that the other man has wheeled transport while he, Jimmy, has nothing but shank's mare.

His neighbour on the plane strolls in to stand beside Jimmy. "You see?" he says. "Conclusive proof. Was it Shakespeare who said whether we ran, walked or crawled, we'd all arrive at death's gate at much the same time? The reason being, we can't enter until the gate opens. Neat, eh? Have you ever observed teenagers pushing and shoving to get into an arena? I've often wondered what would happen if the door opened onto a chasm. What do you think, friend?"

"They'd keep going," Jimmy mutters, as baggage tumbles from the chute onto the carousel.

"That's right. They'd go on. Pressure! Pressure!" The last words are spoken as the chauffeur lifts a large, red-brown leather suitcase from the carousel. He and the other man quickly leave the terminal and walk in the direction of a long, white limousine waiting in an adjacent loading zone.

"I have to go," Jimmy mutters and follows them. The chauffeur puts the suitcase into the car trunk, his passenger enters the rear compartment, the chauffeur gets into the car, starts the motor, and the white monster glides away majestically. Suddenly Jimmy realizes two things: first, he has left his flight bag on the plane; second, unless a miracle occurs, the time, effort and money spent in pursuit of his quarry have been completely in vain. He watches the limousine turn a corner, and at the same time sees a taxi approaching on the other side of the road. Without stopping to think what might happen, Jimmy leaps from the sidewalk and careens through the traffic, waving his arms at the cruising taxi. The driver jams on his brakes, and Jimmy scrambles into the cab beside him.

"Trying to commit suicide?"

"A white limo just left," Jimmy pants.

"White limos are as common as bird shit in LA," the driver tells him.

"Go after it. This is important."

Impelled by the urgency in Jimmy's voice, the driver makes a U-turn in front of screeching oncoming cars. "You playing cops and robbers or what?"

"Murder," Jimmy tersely informs him.

"You been watching too much TV. Where you from?"

"Canada." The driver shrugs as if that explains Jimmy's behaviour. "Can you see the car?"

"Just tell me where you wanna go, pal, and I'll get you there."

"There! There! I see it!" Jimmy points ahead to where the white giant rolls along in the midst of attendant automotive dwarfs.

"How'd you know that's the one?"

"I remember the licence number. Follow it."

The driver sighs, but moves up in traffic until he is positioned a couple of cars behind the white limousine. "Got enough dough to pay for this, pal?"

"Of course. Where do you think they're headed?"

"Probably Beverly Hills. That's where most limos roost." They now leave the flat coastal plain to enter palm tree–lined streets that wind through small valleys. "You are now looking at proof of financial success and movie stardom," the driver announces. "What's your racket, pal?" he asks.

"I'm a lawyer," replies Jimmy.

"Oh jeez! Another one!" the driver says. "Listen man, we've got enough lawyers right here in LA to match every crime ever committed. We got lawyers for crimes that ain't been committed yet. We've even got ones who'll manufacture a crime if they're hard up for one. Man, shortage of crime don't stop lawyers in LA—we got reservoirs of 'em." They round a bend in the road to see the white car pass between mammoth, scrolled gates and vanish around a curve in the driveway as the gates slowly and implacably close. The driver stops his taxi and looks at Jimmy. "Want me to wait while you make a little social call?"

"No."

"Want me to leave you here?"

"Yes."

The driver nods and looks at Jimmy as though he is mentally deficient. "Long walk back."

"I'll be fine."

"Well, this here is the land of the free, so I guess you can do as you please. Anyway, this little jaunt's going to cost you thirty-seven dollars and eighty-two cents."

Jimmy takes out his wallet and hands the driver fifty dollars. "Keep the change."

"Mucho gracias. Hey, want to know something? I'm a lawyer too."

"So, why're you driving a cab?"

"Simple, man, it's real simple. There's already too many flies on the available shit in this burg." The driver-lawyer looks concerned. "Sure you want to get out? I mean, I gotta go back to the airport anyway, so why not tag along?"

"No thanks." Jimmy opens the door.

The driver leans across the seat. "I'm warning you, pal, if the Beverly Hills cops find you wandering around here they'll pick you up faster than a premature ejaculator on a date with a hot starlet. This here's sacred ground, man. You don't buy a shack out here, you buy status. See what I mean? There's a bunch of cops around here who're paid just to make sure guys like you and me don't snoop around. If they see you, pal, they're going to be real suspicious. You want to move around in Beverly Hills, man, you gotta get yourself a BMW or a Porsche, something that'll blend you into the scenery. Listen, man, no offence, but this just ain't your natural environment. The guys who live here will cut each other's throats for another million bucks. I doubt if you're in that league, pal. I sure as hell ain't, so why don't you and me go back to the airport so's you can fly back to little ole Canada where them little ole Mounties always gets their man. How about it?"

When Jimmy continues to shake his head, the driver-lawyer shrugs, as people often do when they feel they have done everything in their power to prevent someone from making a terrible mistake. Then he gestures goodbye, swings his car around and drives away, leaving Jimmy looking glumly at the iron gate and the high, chain-linked fence that appears to enclose the entire property. He experiences an attack of panic and starts to run down the road, hoping the taxi driver is waiting for him around the first bend. But pride asserts itself before he reaches the curve, and he turns and walks resolutely back, past the front gates, around another curve to a point where a bush and tree–filled gorge appears to split the hillside.

Without stopping to think, Jimmy crosses the road and plunges into the gorge like a frightened groundhog skittering down a hole. He finds himself in a narrow rock cleft where the walls rise perhaps twenty-five metres and which is so narrow that bushes and eucalyptus at the top produce a permanent twilight at the bottom. It is quiet, and the dense, warm air is heavily scented with eucalyptus oil from fallen leaves. Jimmy sits with his back against a rock and looks up at the rim, which borders the property where he supposes Janet MacDougail is secluded.

As he examines the rock face and calculates the problems he may have climbing it, doubt creeps in to sap Jimmy's confidence. He suddenly perceives his precipitous flight to Los Angeles may prove nothing more than his own calamitous lack of good sense and judgment. What evidence does he have that Janet is here? Nothing but a few words spoken by the man who is now comfortably seated in the house, probably sipping a pre-luncheon martini and chatting with his family.

Lunch! The word reminds Jimmy that he is hungry, which in turn causes rumbling and churning in his gut. He sits there, wishing himself back in Vancouver, but since he is here, sitting in a gorge outside the fence which surrounds the property where he believes the person he loves is being held against her will, there is no choice but to scale the rock face, climb over the fence and attempt to enter the house. He views his desperate situation as his last gasp, like the final bet made by an obsessive gambler before all is lost and he blows his brains out.

Jimmy yawns and the scented air entering his nostrils resurrects memories from childhood. He sees himself with Julie and Lucille lying on Annette's bed while she vigorously massages them with fragrant oil. The rite has something to do with Annette's belief that the absorption of oils by the skin prevents cold and flu germs from invading their bodies. They giggle hysterically while Annette's fingers probe their sensitive flesh. They wave their legs in the air, and when the plump lips of the girls' vulvas open, Jimmy glimpses the pink tips of their little hooded shafts. He remembers how Annette used to examine their bodies with maternal ferocity, mercilessly flipping them over to part their buttocks in order to make sure there was no evidence of internal worms around their small anuses.

Why is it, Jimmy wonders, that memories flood his mind at inopportune moments? Here he sits recalling the past at a time when he ought to be planning what to do next. It is all a product of the eucalyptus leaves, whose scent lies on the air like flower petals on still water. He recalls his sexual ignorance, the shock of his first bedroom encounter with Evelyn Chan when her sleeve of warm flesh descended and convulsed around his penis. He had never imagined female flesh could be so silken and yet so strong. Nowadays experience enables him to extract a maximum amount of pleasure from his encounters with Evelyn Chan. But maybe that is not true, he thinks, maybe no amount of knowledge and experience would enable him to surpass what he felt that first afternoon with her.

Jimmy dozes and awakens. The images change and he sees Julie lying against him, smearing damp, soft kisses on his face. For a short while Julie had crept into his bed at night to test her emerging sexuality, feeling safe in his presence. Jimmy now feels the points of Julie's eager young breasts pressing against him and his awakened penis prodding the curve of her belly. What might have happened if he had exploited this opportunity? Was it innocence, or was it maternal authority that held them motionless until Julie finally whispered "I'll go now," and slipped away to the bed she shared with Lucille? In reflecting on the memory, Jimmy thinks Julie's nocturnal visits may have had nothing to do with her maturing body, but were simply a continuation of her childish habit of seeking reassurance from her brother after awakening from a frightening dream. It must have been that, because when the mind and emotions of a young woman eventually took possession of Julie's maturing body, visits to his bedroom ceased.

Jimmy finds it strange that his brain has absorbed increments from every micro-second of his life, has filtered, then stored them in remote regions of his mind so that now they require special signals and keys in order to be released and identified in the light of conscious memory. And no doubt his most inaccessible memories cover the years of his early childhood when a man, who later died multiple deaths, had lived with them in the house on Union Street and slept in the marital bed where he pulsed the semen which helped to create three children in Annette's womb. So why cannot Jimmy remember this man? Jimmy thinks that perhaps immense anger blocks all memory of him, that in his unconscious mind he has decided that since the father gave nothing, the father shall be as nothing to the son. Nothing. No memories of a face, or a hand patting a final departure on his head. Just nothing. A void.

Jimmy yawns, stands, stretches, crosses the little gorge, grips the projecting rocks and almost absent-mindedly begins climbing the rock face. He has never climbed rocks or even a tree in his life, yet he has no trouble ascending the cliff. He reaches the top and cautiously peeps over the rim. Directly inside the fence he can see a row of shrubs, and beyond that a diving board and tubular rails, which must be part of a ladder at the deep end of the pool. A high brick wall surrounds the area on three sides, and at the end where the diving board is located Jimmy can see a solid door set into the wall.

He is about to pull himself up and stand by the fence to get a better look, when the door opens and two young women wearing maid's uniforms enter and close the door after them. From the colour of their skins and their black hair, Jimmy supposes they originated in some Latin American country. They quietly talk; when one speaks, the other turns her head to listen attentively. After looking at the water, they sit on the diving board and smoke a cigarette, sharing it puff for puff. Jimmy cannot hear what they are saying and wonders if they are talking about distant families and lovers. When their cigarette is finished they climb onto the board, walk to the end and giggle as they hold hands and bounce, pretending they are about to fall into the water. He watches intently as they walk back and climb from the diving board, stroll slowly around the pool and depart, leaving the door open behind them.

Now Jimmy can look through the pool entrance and see the roof and upper storeys of a large house. The ledge he is standing on is wide enough for him to sit and so he remains there, waiting for darkness to creep over the eastern mountains and down the slopes to blanket the plains and beaches that border the Pacific ocean.

After a couple of hours, he pulls himself up over the rim to stand by the fence. As he does so, lights come on everywhere. For a moment he is poised to drop back down over the rim, but then realizes the property lights must automatically turn on at dusk. He climbs over the fence and drops to the ground. The swimming pool itself is small and utilitarian, and it occurs to Jimmy that it might have been built especially for employees, a perquisite one could expect from an employer in a city where the dreams of even the most lowly servants are occasionally transformed into reality. He walks to the gate and looks across a wide lawn to a house, surrounded by terraces, that at a distance appears to be three or four times larger than the MacDougall house in Vancouver.

Jimmy knows it would be impossible for him to enter the

place surreptitiously. The best he will be able to do is knock on the front door, ask to speak to the man he has followed from Vancouver and explain why he is there. He decides to go ahead with this plan and walks through the door in the wall leading from the pool. As he does so, two men appear, one on each side, to grab his arms, pull them backwards and force him to lean forward.

"Okay, chink," a voice on his right side says. "Move." The men frog-march him along paths to the house, then, once inside, along passages to a small, chilly, windowless room where they push him against a wall. One of the men is the chauffeur Jimmy had seen at the airport, although he no longer wears his white uniform; the other looks as if he could be a Mexican weight lifter. "Looking for anything special?" the chauffeur asks sarcastically. When Jimmy does not reply, he says, "Try him in Spanish, José. Maybe he's a Mexican chink or a goddamn Filipino." In truth, Jimmy cannot speak, because his own ineptitude has left him (temporarily) speechless. Maybe the two maids he had thought so charming and innocent had been ordered to reconnoitre the area and leave the door open when they left.

"I guess we'll have to teach him a few things, eh José?"

"He gotta learn sometime," José agrees.

"You bet he does." The chauffeur steps forward and smacks Jimmy's face, first one side, then the other. Jimmy, who has never been struck so heavily before, finds he is both intimidated and enraged. "Listen, you stupid chink, tell us why you're snooping around. Real fast! You dig?" The blows are repeated, and Jimmy's nose starts to bleed.

"Leave me alone," Jimmy manages to say. He can feel his lips trembling as he wipes blood off them with the back of his hand.

"Hey, José, he can talk. And English too. Ain't that somethin'?"

"I insist on seeing the owner of this house," Jimmy says, trying to sniff blood back up his nose.

"Oh you do, huh? Whadda you want, to do his laundry?"

"Tell your boss I'm here from Vancouver . . . that I saw him there, talking to somebody at the MacDougail's house."

The men look at each other, then at Jimmy, and leave the room, locking the door after them. In a few minutes the door opens again and the chauffeur crooks a finger at Jimmy. He obeys the command and follows, thinking how rapidly captivity produces obedience in prisoners. He is marched through a kitchen, where the women he had watched earlier at the pool stand beside a table and observe his passage, then through a large dining room, across a wide hall and into a book-lined room. There he sees the man he has followed from Vancouver, standing beside a bookcase holding an open volume.

"Let him go," he says and walks across the room to look at Jimmy. "What is your name? And why are you trespassing on my property?"

Jimmy sniffs and wipes more blood from his lips. "James Sung. I'm a lawyer from Vancouver."

The man turns to the chauffeur. "Make sure he stays right here," he says. "And get something to wipe his face." He leaves the room.

"Get him some kleenex, José." José goes out and soon returns with a box of tissues which he tosses at Jimmy.

"Thanks," says Jimmy, ever polite, though failing to catch the box. He picks it up off the lush carpet, extracts tissues and wipes the blood from his lips and nose. Then he moves along the bookcases, looking at the titles. What he sees, the quantity of books and the breadth of subject matter, astonishes him, although he tells himself the man has probably purchased an estate library and uses the books to impress visitors. He continues to scan the shelves until the man returns.

"I've arranged for your return to Vancouver," the man says. "You will leave now. Go with these men. They will take you to the airport."

"I am here to get Janet MacDougail."

The man looks at his watch. "There is no person of that name in this house. Now, if you have any sense at all, you will make no further trouble. You may not be a fool, Mr. Sung, but undoubtedly you are misguided."

"I think you are lying."

The man angrily walks the length of the room and returns to stand before Jimmy. "Let us understand something quite clearly, Mr. Sung. When I give my word to another person, I am believed, because people with far greater experience than you possess know I never lie or break my word. Therefore, when I tell you Janet MacDougail is not in this house, you would be wise to take me at my word. Do you understand me, Mr. Sung?"

"Then where is she?"

"I have no idea."

"But you were at the MacDougail house in Vancouver yesterday. I saw you there. Are you going to tell me Mrs. MacDougail didn't discuss the death of her grandson with you?"

"What I discuss with other people is none of your business, Mr. Sung. Now, you are either going to leave quietly with these men, or I will telephone the police and tell them you have illegally entered my property. Make no mistake about it, Mr. Sung, there will be no question whom the police will believe." He turns away as the chauffeur approaches Jimmy and takes his arm.

"Take your goddamn hands off me!" Jimmy shouts.

"Don't touch him, Robert," the man says. "Just make sure he gets onto the plane."

The chauffeur grotesquely grins at Jimmy. "Please come this way, sir."

Jimmy strides stiff-legged from the room, following directions given him by the chauffeur, who stalks directly behind him. They pass through the kitchen, where a number of women are gathered around the big, central table on which dishes of food have been set out. Two of the women are young, tall and blonde-haired, southern California *sui generis*, probably hired for some after dinner kinkiness. They glance at Jimmy as he passes, and then return to matters of greater importance.

In the garage sit four luxury cars, one being the white

limousine. "Hey, José, it's kind of weird driving this goof in the limo."

"We got no choice. Need the two Mercedes for the putas, and we never touch boss's Maserati."

"Let's stuff this chop suey asshole in the trunk."

"The boss he no like that."

Jimmy had never though much of Mexicans before but suddenly figures they must be good people.

José opens the door of the limousine, and as Jimmy leans forward to enter the car Robert, having been thwarted, kicks his behind. Jimmy sprawls across the car's interior and hits his head on the opposite door, which fortunately for him is heavily padded.

"Don't bother trying to skip out at the stop lights, dickhead, because the doors is locked." The two men position themselves in the front seat.

In smooth, silent and ironic luxury Jimmy is conveyed through the dim Beverly Hills valley and across the glittering Los Angeles plains to the airport, where the chauffeur collects a boarding pass before he and José walk him to the security gate.

"Know what I'd do with this guy, José, if I was the pilot? I'd fly over the ocean, open a door and chuck him out. There's too many goddamn chinks in the world already, right José?" Naturally, José agrees. At security, they let Jimmy loose and watch until he is out of sight.

Once Jimmy reaches the boarding area and shows his pass, the flight attendant hurries him along the ramp to the plane. "As a rule, we don't hold up a departure for anybody but senators," she tells Jimmy. "So you must be a very important person."

"I suppose I am," Jimmy admits as they enter the plane and he is shown to a first-class seat. Of course he is important, Jimmy tells himself . . . as an animal is important to a person about to dispose of it. But wait! Yes, he *is* important: for the past few hours he has been a focal point in the life of his unwitting quarry and he is precious cargo now to an elegant flight attendant until the plane lands in Vancouver. The attendant lavishes Jimmy with attention and circumventious questions. When Jimmy admits he is hungry she says: "I guess you were too busy today to eat. What kind of day was it?"

Jimmy searches for an appropriate adjective to describe his day. Finally he says, "It has truly been . . . Faustian."

"Oh," and she giggles.

Jimmy rapidly swallows glasses of California champagne and empties the plates of delicious food the flight attendant places before him. Before long he finds he can believe that nothing in the world matters except to experience pleasures powerful enough to obliterate memory and transcend pain. He imagines himself flying on and on until he and everything in the firmament are finally evaporated into a triumphant black void. He remembers his fellow passenger on the flight from Vancouver gratuitously delivering a dissertation on the socially destructive nature of transportation systems, and when the attendant solicitously leans over him to ask if he wants more champagne, he has an impulse to put an arm around her hips and warn her of the man's gloomy prognosis for the future of humanity. He wants to tell her that the electronic age with its swarming epidemic of computers is certainly going to be the final step into oblivion, and instead of going to Vancouver, she should fly away with him to a tropical destination, there to recline beneath a palm tree, gathering rosebuds, sipping champagne and forgetting about time's chariot looming ever closer. But by the time Jimmy has formulated how to say all this, she has moved on to another passenger and Jimmy realizes he is tipsy.

The plane begins its descent into Vancouver and the precursor of a hangover asserts itself in the form of a throbbing headache. As the incline of the plane increases, the bile in Jimmy's throat rises, and when the wheels of the plane finally screech on the runway, the combination of bile, champagne and bits of undigested food hits the roof of his mouth and then rushes back through his esophagus into his heaving stomach.

"We're here, Mr. Sung," the flight attendant tells the

recumbent Jimmy, who levers himself from the cushions, weaves past her and rushes from the plane into the first wash-room he finds (it has a female icon on the door) where he ejects the contents of his stomach before continuing on through the almost deserted terminal to collapse in the back seat of a taxi.

"Rough trip, eh?" the cabbie says.

"Very," whispers Jimmy, "very."

10

Annette cautiously peers around the door before removing the chain to let Jimmy into the house. She says she will make him a pot of tea before returning to bed, ignoring protests that he does not want it. While waiting for the kettle to boil, she produces a bottle of ginseng preparation, pours out a tablespoonful and orders Jimmy to swallow it. "All this tearing around upsets the system," she says. To avoid argument Jimmy does as he is told.

They sit at the kitchen table listening to the movements of the water in the kettle without saying anything. Just as the kettle is about to boil, Annette speaks. "Uncle Jimmy telephoned."

"So, what's new about that?" Jimmy glumly asks.

"He says you're wasting your time running around looking for Janet."

"It's my time," Jimmy says. As Annette puts the pot of tea and a cup on the table, he realizes the only way his uncle could have known he was searching for Janet is if Annette told him. "Did you say anything to Uncle Jimmy about what I was doing, Mother?"

"No," Annette says.

"Then how does he know?"

Annette shrugs, then says, "Anyway, it's no big deal. I'm going back to bed." She goes to the kitchen entrance.

"Just a minute, Mother." Annette halts in the doorway. "You're quite sure you didn't tell him I'd gone to Los Angeles?"

"I didn't tell anybody."

"Do you remember his exact words?"

"He said you were wasting your time looking for Janet. I've explained that, Jimmy."

"This could be important, Mother. Had you been talking about Janet?"

"I don't know . . . I don't remember. Maybe I told him you were upset . . . you were upset, weren't you? So what's the big deal in telling Uncle Jimmy you're upset?"

"I don't understand you, Mother. I asked you specifically not to tell anyone, especially Uncle Jimmy, where I was going or what I was doing."

"I didn't."

"I'll bet you said enough that he could put two and two together. Isn't that what happened?" Annette shakes her head and turns to leave. "Well, it doesn't matter now." Jimmy listens to his mother slowly climbing the stairs and closing her bedroom door. He knows he needs sleep and should go to bed. Instead he continues to sit at the table, staring at the untouched tea, thick-headed, confused and depressed. He asks himself why some people (notably himself) appear always to make wrong choices—tearing off to Los Angeles is a good example. He has made a fool of himself by falling in love with a girl whose family wants nothing to do with him, and on top of that he has failed to do what he promised her, namely, to provide a reasonable explanation of her brother's death. Really, if he had any sense he would close down his office for good and work in Annette's store. Eventually he goes to bed where he turns restlessly before falling into the pit of chaotic, dream-filled sleep. He is awakened by the persistent ringing of the phone in the kitchen below and is shocked when he glances at the clock to discover it is the middle of the next afternoon. When the phone continues to ring, he goes down to answer it.

It is Sergeant Robson. "I guess some guys get to laze away the day in bed while the rest of us jerks are out in the world, slaving away."

"What do you want?" Jimmy asks, through a prolonged yawn.

"Want! I don't want anything. Except a couple of months away from dead bodies—like the one I'm looking at right now."

"Isn't that part of your job? Why tell me about it?"

"I thought you'd be interested in this body. It's Victor Cranley's. I'm in the apartment with his body now."

"Cranley!"

"That's right. Murdered. Some joker shot him. I don't suppose you know anything about it, eh Mr. Sung?"

"That's not funny, Sergeant."

"You bet it isn't. Especially for Victor Cranley. Well . . . see you around."

"Wait. How long you going to be there?"

"Oh, maybe another hour. Depends on what I turn up."

"Mind if I join you?"

"Why should I?" Robson hangs up. Jimmy returns to his room, dresses hurriedly, then checks to see if Annette's car is available. On the way out the kitchen door he collects a couple of apples and eats them while driving to the Point Grey apartment building where a police officer gets an okay from Robson before letting him in.

"They've taken him away," Robson tells Jimmy as he enters the basement suite. "Cranley was sitting in that arm chair there, looking at the TV. It was still on. Somebody shot him in the chest. Close up. With a small calibre gun. Any ideas who might have done it, Mr. Sung?"

"None." Jimmy glances around the room at the furniture, which looks as though it was purchased thirty years ago.

"Where were you yesterday, Mr. Sung?"

"In Los Angeles."

"Breezed off to Disneyland, eh?"

"I was there on business. I left in the morning and came back on a late flight."

Robson does not pursue Jimmy's trip to Los Angeles. "You think maybe our friend with the lisp killed Victor Cranley?"

Jimmy hesitates. It would be a convenient solution. "It's

a possibility," he says, "though would Cranley have invited him into his suite?"

"Maybe not. But I ask myself, why would somebody go to the trouble of killing a harmless old guy like Cranley? And the only explanation I can come up with—apart from the murderer being a raving lunatic—is because Cranley's the guy who let Lisp into Martin's apartment. In fact he's the only guy we know of who ever saw Lisp—except for Janet McDougail."

"That may be too simple an explanation, Sergeant."

"I'll tell you something about homicides, Mr. Sung. Most *are* simple. Complicated ones are found only in books. So . . . Cranley's sitting in his arm chair looking at a cops and robbers show, his buzzer goes, he identifies the person, unlatches the doors and goes back to his TV show. The person walks in, says hello, leans over, shoots him in the chest, and walks out. Nobody in the building hears a bloody thing—televisions are on, apartment doors are closed, and small calibre guns don't make much noise. So let's bring a little simplicity into our lives, Mr. Sung. Okay? Let's not make things more complicated than they naturally are. Come on, let's look around, eh?"

Jimmy watches while Robson searches the immaculately neat suite. "Christ, I hate doing this," Robson exclaims as he looks in the bedroom closet where Cranley's dead wife's clothes still hang. He picks up and puts down a photograph of Cranley's wife on which Cranley had written *I never realized I would miss you so much.*

"Something has occurred to me, Sergeant," Jimmy says. "Suppose the man who lisps doesn't actually exist?"

"Hell . . . Cranley identified him, and the MacDougail girl claims when he looked at her she got goose bumps on her bottom."

"I'm not suggesting the man doesn't exist—only that he doesn't usually lisp."

"Hm! I've thought of that possibility too, Mr. Sung." Robson opens a dresser drawer and takes out a package of letters bound with ribbon. "Ever receive a love letter?" Jimmy shakes his head. Robson drops the letters into the drawer and closes it. "Gone out of fashion, eh? You know, if the lisp is a put-on, then the guy's still walking around Vancouver."

"And if Janet saw him, that means she could be in danger."

"She could be. Maybe that's why her family spirited her away. What d'you think of that theory, Mr. Sung?"

"It's possible," Jimmy admits.

"Trouble is, anything's possible—and where does that get us? Let's go, I can't do anything more here." Jimmy follows Robson out of the building and they stand on the sunlit pavement near Robson's car. "I suppose with any luck we'll clear things up eventually." Robson opens the car door, then turns as if suddenly remembering something. "There's something I've been meaning to ask you, Mr. Sung. Your father's dead, isn't he?"

"Yes," Jimmy tersely replies. "A logging accident."

"Hm!" Robson shakes his head. "Your mother came to Canada around 1950, didn't she?"

"I'm not sure the exact year. Why do you want to know?"

"Oh, curiosity. You happen to know her family name?"

Jimmy attempts to produce a light, easy laugh. "All I know is Mother was separated from her family when she was a girl, when the fighting between the Communists and the Kuomintang was going on. Why do you ask?"

"I've received another informative communique about the MacDougail family from the FBI. Jeez! Those guys sure have tags on everybody."

"What's your point, Sergeant?"

"Ah yes . . . the point. Well, the point is this. Remember I mentioned how the MacDougail family funds an orphan adoption agency? It really beats me how the FBI manages to get this kind of information. But anyway, there's a list of children the agency brought into the States and Canada—mostly kids from Asia—and among them there's one Annette Li."

"I don't know what you're driving at, Sergeant," Jimmy mutters.

"The interesting point is, Mr. Sung, the girl Annette was sponsored into the home of one James Sung, who is listed as being a director of the Northwest Paper Company, which—big surprise—turns out to be a subsidiary of MacDougail, Inc."

"The girl couldn't have been Mother. She met and married my father in Hong Kong, I'm quite sure of that. She still has her Hong Kong passport, though she's a Canadian citizen now."

Robson shrugs. "Well, it's probably coincidence."

"I'm sure it is. Li is a fairly common Chinese name."

"Hm!." Robson opens the car door wider. "Oh . . . something else . . . . It's about the dead body those kids found in Burnaby." Jimmy nods. "Turns out it's William MacDougail. Death from natural causes—if cirrhosis of the liver and starvation can be called natural causes. And one more point. William MacDougail owned the house he died in and the market-garden land around it. Funny, eh? Carrots and god knows what else growing up to his front door—and he starves to death. Beats me. I'll be in touch, Mr. Sung." He drives away, leaving Jimmy standing on the pavement desperately striving to rearrange everything he knows about the past.

Jimmy is so disturbed by the information given him by Robson he is unaware he is walking in the opposite direction from where he parked the car. He thinks there must be an explanation for what Robson has told him but cannot think what it might be. He begins to hate Robson, seeing him as a sadistic bully, extracting pleasure from knowing how disturbed Jimmy is bound to be after being asked questions about his mother. He decides that Robson has been stringing him along, pretending geniality and exuding goodwill, when he really believes that Jimmy is implicated in the deaths of three people because of a yet-to-be proven connection between the Sung and MacDougail families. What if Robson has been manipulating him all along in an attempt to get at the murderers, and maybe at drug traffickers, through him? Would such a thing be possible? Does this also mean that Robson suspects Annette of wrongdoing?

Jimmy is so horrified at the direction his speculations are taking him he halts and stares fixedly at a house across the street as if answers to the questions flooding his mind will be found behind its windows. Abruptly he turns and walks back until he finds himself standing beside the white Corolla. He enters the car and sits there, staring at the steering wheel, knowing he has to drive somewhere, though he cannot bring himself either to go home or to the store. He does not want to see Annette, afraid she will return lies to his questions, so he makes up his mind to visit Evelyn Chan. He drives through the car-filled streets, parks, goes up the stairs to her townhouse and rings the doorbell. But as he presses the button, he panics because he realizes he will not be able to supply a convincing explanation for coming on an unscheduled day. He turns and runs along the sidewalk as Evelyn Chan opens the door. "Why, Jimmy . . . what . . .?"

"It doesn't matter," Jimmy calls to the wind. "It doesn't matter."

She calls to Jimmy, but he has reached his car and now wrenches the door open, scrambles in, starts the motor, and speeds along the street, passing Evelyn Chan who watches him drive by, eyes and mouth wide with surprise. Jimmy ends up at the store, during the brief drive having made up his mind he is going to force the truth from Annette's lips. Unfortunately he is not able to carry out his plan because customers fill the store and Annette and Lucille are busily serving them. On seeing Jimmy, Lucille curtly orders him to help, and Jimmy, in appearance at least, still a dutiful son, falls to. Later, during the evening meal, he still cannot bring himself to question Annette. Instead he covertly watches her, wondering how many lies she has told him over the years. He is upset and has difficulty eating. His head aches, and after brushing aside Annette's offer of a glass of her special cure-all, he swallows several aspirin and goes to bed.

When he awakens in the morning his headache is accompanied by a fever and sore throat. He remains in bed, drifting feverishly in and out of sleep, until Annette comes home and persuades him to drink a glass of her elixir, all the while telling him he wouldn't be sick if he had taken it the night before. Later in the afternoon, Annette's curative mixture drives Jimmy to the bathroom where it scours his intestines as he sits trembling on the toilet. He staggers back to bed where he dreams he is free-falling off an impossibly high cliff into the arms of a composite of Annette, Evelyn Chan, Lucille and Janet. He drifts into wakefulness to hear Lucille's voice demanding to know why he is groaning. "Awful dream," Jimmy whispers.

"Serves you right for being sick. Mother says I'm to give you more aspirin and something to drink." When Jimmy whispers that all he wants to do is die, Lucille says, "Good riddance. It's your own fault for flying off to Pouce Coupé."

On the second day, Lucille tells Jimmy if he is not better soon Annette is going to get Doctor Wong—a herbalist, naturopath and regular customer of Annette's—to come in and examine him. The spectre of ingesting one of Doctor Wong's concoctions may have the effect of hastening Jimmy's recovery, because on the third day he awakens feeling much better, although his knees still quiver when he weaves from his bed to the bathroom. Annette is delighted; she is convinced his recovery is due entirely to her special potion. Jimmy weakly smiles as the questions he wants to ask Annette churn unspoken in his head.

Before she goes to the store, Jimmy asks her to leave the Corolla for him to drive to the office and sort his mail. Although Annette tells Jimmy he should rest in bed for another day and that she can collect his mail, she finally agrees to leave the car. On her way out the door, Annette turns to smile at Jimmy, and he realizes with a poignancy aggravated by his physical weakness how deeply his mother and sisters care for him. He remembers during his childhood and adolescence how Annette encouraged and admonished him, and how his sisters turned to him for help with their lessons or for reassurance after quarrelling with a friend. He remembers Janet too, on that first occasion, sitting in his office, mixing lapses into childish behaviour with pretensions of adult assurance, while digging the tunnel which eventually undermined and collapsed his professional defences. Even now, he can recall an image of her as she slumped sideways in the office chair, chewing her lips, one long leg crossed over the other to expose honey-coloured thighs. He wishes she had never found his name in the Yellow Pages and speculates on what might have happened had she gone to another agency, but ends by thinking she was fated to visit him, as he was fated to fall in love with her. Frightened that the thoughts concerning the investigation which have been swarming in his head during the past few days will be confirmed by future events, he forces himself to get up, bathe and dress, eat a little of the food Annette has prepared for him and drive to the store, where his mother's greeting combines love, worry and an order that while he is permitted to pick up his mail, he must go home to read it. Jimmy nods, slowly climbs the stairs to his office and sifts through his mail. He discards all of it until the pile is reduced to one envelope with a hand-written address. He opens the envelope and reads the letter inside it.

May 15

Dear Mr. Sung:

I hope you won't mind me writing a letter to you, but somebody should know about an experience I had yesterday. As you can imagine, I don't want to have anything to do with the police after the way they treated me. I heard the Sergeant call you Mr. Sung, and it was easy to find your name and address in the phone book. It was then I realized you are a private investigator.

You know, Mr. Sung, I lost my wife last year, and since then I've been upset and nervous, because we were married for over forty years, and when you lose someone who means so much to you, you feel half your life is gone. Before she died I promised her I wouldn't sit around in our suite all day and mope but would get out into the shopping malls to mingle with other people. My wife and I always did our shopping at Oakridge Mall, so that's where I go. My wife bought her bath soap at a special shop there, and so I often sit on a bench across from that shop and watch people pass by. That's where I was sitting when I saw that young man I let into Mr. MacDougail's apartment.

He was at the rear of the shop, and all I saw was his profile, but I'm sure it was him. I waited on the bench so I could get a good look at him when he came out, but that didn't happen. He never came out. This is what I don't understand. Where did he go? I suppose I could have made a mistake, but I don't think so. Anyway, I thought I'd let you know I saw him.

Yours truly,
Victor Cranley

Jimmy looks at the postmark on the envelope and notes it is dated the day he flew to Los Angeles. The letter disturbs Jimmy because he senses Cranley's loneliness might explain his obsequious behaviour the day Robson questioned him. Jimmy feels guilty because he stood by and allowed Robson to bully a man so transparently innocent of any wrongdoing, a man who is now dead, having gone to his death feeling besmirched by the police force he had been taught to respect all his life.

Jimmy rereads the letter and strives to grasp its implications, but the information only adds to his confusion and he ends up telling himself that Cranley must have been mistaken. Still, he dials Robson's number and is surprised when Robson actually answers it.

When Jimmy tells Robson about the letter, he says, "Hm! I'll be right over. I want to see it."

Jimmy sits numbly and waits. Before long he hears Robson's loud voice say, "Hello there, Mrs. Sung. Produce stands still out on the sidewalk, eh?" He listens to the sound of Robson's heavy footsteps on the stairs and automatically counts them. Robson plods along the passage and enters the office eating an apple Annette has given him. He does not greet Jimmy, but takes up the letter and reads it. "Hm!" he mutters a couple of times, then puts the letter down and eyes Jimmy. "What the hell's wrong with you?"

"Flu," Jimmy replies, reducing the volume of his voice to a tubercular whisper.

"Lots of it around," Robson comments as he puts the apple

core on Jimmy's desk. "So what d'you think, Mr. Sung? Did Cranley actually see Lisp?" Jimmy raises his shoulders to signify uncertainty. "Hm! Probably mistaken identity. We run up against it all the time. Anyway, I'll take the letter and make a copy of it. That okay with you?" Jimmy nods. Robson crosses the room to stand at the window. "Had any ideas about Cranley's murderer?"

"I've been too sick to think about anything."

"Goddamn it, why didn't Cranley give us a call?"

"He didn't trust you."

"Okay, okay. He was probably mistaken anyway."

"If he was, then why was he shot? Look . . . Cranley spots someone he's sure is Lisp. He goes home, writes and mails a letter, then a day or so later is shot to death. There's a pattern in all this, Sergeant. I meet and question Betty Nelson and she dies. I get a letter from Cranley and he dies."

"Hm! Did you tell anyone you'd talked to Betty Nelson?"

"I mentioned it to Janet, but she had never heard of her."

"Okay. Let's go over everything again. First you find Betty Nelson's body. Then we talk some. We go to Martin MacDougail's apartment. We talk to Cranley who tells us about Lisp. I come here and interview the MacDougail girl who says she once saw a guy who lisps and doesn't like him because he has X-ray eyes. So what does it all add up to, eh?"

"I should point out, Sergeant, you were convinced Janet was lying when she told you about seeing Lisp with her brother."

"Well, I could have been mistaken. It wouldn't be the first time. Then what happens? Cranley goes to Oakridge, sits on a bench and thinks he sees Lisp's head in a store—and instead of getting in touch with the police, he writes that letter to you."

"We've already covered this ground, Sergeant."

"Then we'll cover it again, Mr. Sung . . . and again . . . as many times as I think necessary. Okay, then Cranley is shot. So, what's the link in these deaths? The link, Mr. Sung, is you."

"Now you are going too far, Sergeant."

"I said *link*, not perpetrator. So—why would two people be killed after you talked to them, Mr. Sung?"

"To prevent me—and the police—from finding out who killed Martin MacDougail. But don't forget I had no part in questioning Cranley. Your link theory breaks down there."

"Not necessarily. Did you ever say anything to Janet MacDougail about Cranley?"

"I don't think so."

"Hm!" Robson walks from the window to the desk, stares at Jimmy a few seconds, then returns to the window. "Why does so much in this case connect you and the girl? Got an explanation for that?"

"I suppose because Janet originally brought me into the investigation. I can't think of any other reason."

"Neither can I. Tell me more about your first meeting with her. What exactly did she say that day?"

"Oh . . . let me see . . . . She was dissatisfied with the police's explanation of her brother's death. She was convinced he would never commit suicide."

"How could she know that?"

"You want to know what she told me?"

"Yeah. Go on."

"Since she can't believe her brother killed himself, she wants somebody besides the police to investigate his death. Later I offer to drive her home, and as we're crossing Main and Broadway she tells me that's where she saw her brother talking to a girl. I've already told you all this, Sergeant."

"Yeah, yeah. I know you have. I'm just trying to fit the pieces together."

"But the things Janet told me don't fit in anywhere, Sergeant. They only prove she didn't know much about her brother's life."

"Or that's what she wanted you to believe."

"No. Janet was genuinely shocked when she heard we'd found drugs in Martin's apartment. And she acted the same way when I told her the girl she'd seen Martin talking to on Broadway may have been a prostitute."

"Y'know something, Mr. Sung? I have a problem believing she could be so bloody ignorant."

"It isn't ignorance, Sergeant. Janet idealized Martin. And surely it's not unusual for girls to feel that way about an older brother."

"Okay, so she's dewy-eyed about her brother. But what does that tell us? Bugger-all I can see. Look, somebody besides Martin and Betty Nelson had to know about that house in East Vancouver. And somebody had to know Victor Cranley got a glimpse of Lisp at Oakridge mall. Right? Did you ever mention the house in East Vancouver to Janet?"

"It's possible. But I didn't tell her anything about Cranley being at Oakridge . . . unless . . ." Jimmy's voice trails off. He looks at Robson, wondering if Robson perceives the implications of what he has said.

Robson moves from the window to stand beside Jimmy's desk. "Run out of bright ideas, Mr. Sung?"

"I've run out of the obvious," Jimmy admits.

"So what's left?" Jimmy shakes his head, barely able to contemplate what is left. "A guy who puts on a lisp to identify himself when he's on the job, but fades into the woodwork after the job's done. Right?"

"That's about it," Jimmy agrees.

"I dunno why, but I thought maybe Cranley's letter might supply the answer." Robson grins at Jimmy. "I guess a guy's never too old to indulge in wishful thinking, eh?"

"It's not a culpable crime, Sergeant," Jimmy replies.

"And it's not exactly laudable, either," Robson angrily says, "especially in guys who claim to be professionals." He picks up and gently waves the letter. "I'll have this copied and get it back to you, Mr. Sung."

Robson leaves, and Jimmy listens to his footsteps on the stairs and the sound of his voice mingled with Annette's as his mother (Jimmy is sure of this) hands him a bag of apples. Jimmy pushes himself out of the chair and goes to the window to look down at Annette and Robson as they stand at the edge of the sidewalk. He watches as Robson raises the bag gesturing his thanks, gets into his car and drives away. Jimmy sighs and goes to his desk where he types out two pages on which he presents his solutions to the deaths of Martin MacDougail, Betty Nelson and Victor Cranley. He reads over what he has written, puts it into an envelope and hides it in his filing cabinet, in the same drawer as the girlie magazine. He then goes down to the store where he waits until Annette has finished serving a customer.

After the customer leaves, Annette crosses to where Jimmy stands and asks how he is feeling. "I'm all right," he says. "Mother, will you telephone Uncle Jimmy and tell him I'm on my way over to see him?"

"Why? What d'you want to see him for?"

"Tell him it's concerning MacDougail Incorporated."

"What's that?"

"Look, Mother, either I talk to Uncle or Sergeant Robson will. Robson thinks it'll be easier if I do it. Now, will you please phone and say I'm on my way?"

"You're sure it's no big deal, Jimmy?"

"Only if he wants to make one out of it." Annette hesitates, then goes to the telephone, dials the unlisted number, and after glancing around as if to make sure Jimmy is not moving closer to listen, speaks into the receiver, while Jimmy waits on a couple of customers.

"It's okay," Annette says when she comes back. "But don't stir up more trouble. Understand?"

"Mother . . ." Jimmy begins, then stops because he senses that there is really no point in offering explanations to Annette. Quite the contrary, he concludes. Explanations are due him from Uncle Jimmy, and perhaps from Annette too. "I'll be back soon," he says and sets off along the street on weak legs towards the red-brick building that houses his Uncle Jimmy.

11

In the far-off days of his early childhood Jimmy firmly believed the world was governed by reciprocity and fair play. His belief was cataclysmically destroyed one day when he asked Annette why he and his sisters were never invited to Uncle Jimmy's home while he freely came to theirs. Annette's reply terminated Jimmy's belief in universal give and take.

"He doesn't want us there," she had said.

"Why not?" an indignant Jimmy had responded.

Annette delivered her standard response to any probing question from Jimmy. "I dunno. Anyway, it's no big deal. Nobody is allowed there, except his current girlfriend and the servants, not even Sam Mackintosh."

The upshot of this brief exchange was that whenever the boy Jimmy walked past the block-long red-brick building with two upper floors given over to living quarters for Uncle Jimmy, he looked up and poked out his tongue, thereby demonstrating his long-standing resentment. But, being cautious even in those remote days, Jimmy allowed only the tip of his tongue to protrude, so that if someone were looking from a distance the action would be seen as a child licking his lips; in such fashion had Jimmy watered down his gesture of contempt to one of mild defiance. Later on, during his adolescent years, Jimmy, realizing that sticking out one's tongue to protest man's inhumanity to man is about as ineffectual as waving a placard, negotiated a compromise with himself, deciding to avoid altogether the building where his uncle resides during his sojourns in Vancouver.

The apartment is guarded by an electronically controlled door and grill, into which Jimmy mutters his name. He hears clicks, the door opens and he enters a lobby to face an elevator which has a keyhole but lacks a control panel. He waits while he hears rattles and more clicks behind the elevator door, then the door opens and Jimmy enters a large teak-lined box. The door closes, the elevator slowly rises, stops, the door reopens and Jimmy walks into a hall where Uncle Jimmy waits.

Together they walk from the hall into a room several times larger than the house on Union Street. The coffered ceiling, elaborately plastered, painted and gilded, is over six metres in height. Three of the four walls are covered with paintings and tapestries. The fourth wall consists entirely of windows; beyond them lies the glorious spectacle of Burrard Inlet and the North Shore mountains. Standing in the middle of the room, the floor of which is covered with an immense Chinese carpet, Jimmy thinks he now understands why his uncle reserves the privacy of this magnificent room for himself alone.

"Don't look so surprised, Nephew," Uncle Jimmy says. "I'm not responsible for the decor. My father had the apartment decorated in the thirties and I haven't changed it much since. Good architects and craftspeople were plentiful then, and cheap too. Annette tells me you've been ill."

"I've had the flu." Jimmy crosses the room and looks intently at a painting of a young woman wearing a red dress and brocaded slippers. "That's Lucille!" he exclaims, turning to face his uncle, who has walked over to stand beside him.

"Someone who resembles her."

"It's incredible. I could swear it was Lucille."

"Would you like a drink, Nephew? Since you've not been well, a little brandy might be beneficial." He goes to a cabinet, opens it, pours cognac into two small glasses and returns to hand one to Jimmy. "Annette says you want to discuss something with me. I assume it's a matter of some importance."

"Sergeant Robson wants to know when you became a director of the Northwest Paper Company."

Uncle Jimmy turns and walks to a chair placed near the windows. "I think Sergeant Robson should conduct his own interviews, Nephew."

"Robson thought your answer to the question would be of interest to me," Jimmy says, following his uncle to the windows.

"I fail to see why. Even if I had been a member of the board of directors of a MacDougail company it can have no possible relevance for either you or Sergeant Robson."

"Does that mean Robson's information is not correct?"

"It means you have no right to ask the question, Nephew."

"In that case, I'll leave it to Sergeant Robson to ask you." Jimmy puts the glass of untouched brandy on a table and makes for the entry hall. He knows he is behaving irrationally but cannot prevent years of resentment and anger from erupting to the surface.

"Just a minute, Nephew." Jimmy stops and half-turns to see that his uncle has moved from his position at the windows. "It doesn't follow that because I think you and Robson—who has apparently inveigled you into becoming his errand boy—have no right to question me that I'm not prepared to respond to a question about my business activities, provided I'm given a reason for doing it. Now, why do you want to know if I served as a director of one of the MacDougail companies?"

"Because law enforcement agents in the United States have evidence the MacDougails are involved in the narcotics trade—and because Robson thinks Martin MacDougail was dealing in cocaine." He spits the words out viciously. "That's why!"

"There's no cause to get angry, Nephew. I'm fully aware you resent me, but I must point out my request is perfectly reasonable. Now I've heard your explanation, I have no objection to telling you that I served several terms as a director on the board of the Northwest Paper Company, a subsidiary of MacDougail Incorporated, which owns and operates two pulp-and-paper mills in the province. As a respected businessman

I'm frequently approached to act in a similar capacity." Jimmy and his uncle eye each other with mutual animosity.

"Sergeant Robson will want to know more about your financial involvement with the company."

"I have none. While sitting on the board I was offered the usual honoraria and stock options. I declined the stock options—I'm not interested in trading in the securities market. I own certain properties in various countries in the world and I'm content to limp along, managing these as best I can."

Jimmy scans the beautifully appointed room. "You seem to manage better than most."

"Sarcasm does not become a man whose income hovers on the poverty line, Nephew. Does Sergeant Robson need to know anything more?"

"Yes, he wants to know about someone who immigrated to Canada many years ago. A girl named—" Jimmy stops because a young Oriental woman has entered the room. She is wearing a green dress and her long black hair is dressed in two braids which lie like coiled snakes upon her shoulders. Her movements are languid, exaggerated to the point of artificiality. She looks first at Jimmy, then at James Sung, silently waiting to be introduced.

"This is Marie-Therese," Uncle Jimmy says. Jimmy nods politely. "And this—"

"No, don't tell me. Let me guess," Marie-Therese says with a French accent, embellishing her words with a high, trilling laugh. She points one finger at Jimmy, the other at Uncle Jimmy. "It's your son, the one you talk so much about. He looks just like you. Amazing." She turns to Jimmy. "You know, Jimmy, your father tells me you are a very clever young man. As you must know, there are very few clever people in the world; unfortunately I'm not one of them. Which is a pity, isn't it? I mean, if I were clever I wouldn't be here, would I? Goodbye. It's been a pleasure meeting you." She turns and leaves the room, moving her hips in such a way that the skirt of her dress swings from side to side, gets onto the elevator and then disappears from sight.

Jimmy watches her go, mouth open and slack arms hanging at his sides as if paralyzed. He turns mechanically and looks past the man he has always known as his uncle toward the picture of the woman in the red dress. "That's not Lucille," he manages to say, "it's . . . it's Mother. It's Annette." He mechanically turns his still-stiff body to focus on the man who has been suddenly transformed from a distant relative into his father. "Julie . . . Lucille . . ." The words emerge as a thin, eerie shriek.

"Well, yes . . . but . . ."

"No!" Jimmy shouts. "Mother told us about our father. He . . ." There Jimmy stops because he recognizes the truth.

"You kept asking about your father, so Annette had to invent something . . ."

"You . . . you . . . swine! You swine!" Jimmy wants to vent his rage and smash clenched fists down upon the head of the aging man who now watches him apprehensively. He can hardly bear to think of this man crouched upon his mother in the act of begetting him and his sisters.

James Sung, Senior backs away from his son, goes to the table, and returns with the glass of brandy. "Here. It will help." Jimmy takes the glass, swallows the contents, shudders and violently coughs. His father retrieves the glass, refills it and brings it back.

Jimmy takes the glass, and drinks most of the brandy. "Why? Why? Tell me why!"

The question acts like an explosive on a weakened dam. "You don't understand what she was like . . . to me, she was beautiful. She had no idea where she'd been born . . . where her family came from . . . she remembered nothing. Nothing. People in the orphanage gave her a name."

"Annette Li!" Jimmy exclaims and his father nods.

"Peter MacDougail, who was the CEO of Northwest Paper at the time, was making placements for Asian orphans. He requested my help in finding a home for her in Canada."

"Like the homes you find for other girls?"

"No, no, nothing like that. The women who come to live with me understand why they are here. They have no illusions.

They come to my bed when I need them—much as you go to Evelyn Chan's. And they are well remunerated for their services. But, when I saw Annette . . ."

"How old was she?"

"No one at the orphanage knew her age. She may have been fourteen years old . . . maybe fifteen . . ." Jimmy's father points to the painting. "I commissioned it just after you were born. Annette seemed happy enough then. When she told me she wanted more children I thought it meant she was content with me." He shakes his head, goes to the cabinet, pours more brandy, quickly swallows it, then returns, talking and gesturing as he walks. Even to Jimmy, trapped as he is in a state of tension and confusion, it is apparent that recounting his story is deeply disturbing for his father. "Then one day . . . Lucille was only a baby . . . Annette announced she was leaving me."

"Why didn't you offer to marry her?" Jimmy shouts.

His father shouts back. "You think I didn't? I wanted to! But she wouldn't have me. Don't you get it? Are you such a nincompoop you can't understand that Annette didn't want me! She didn't trust me . . . she didn't trust anybody. I told her I loved her . . . I still do . . . but she wouldn't allow herself to love me." He returns to the cabinet to pour more brandy. "I told Annette I would always protect her . . . but it wasn't enough for her. The only people she felt safe with were the children who had come from her own body. I did try to keep her . . . but it was no use." He suddenly sits, leans back, and closes his eyes as if the outburst has exhausted him.

"Are you all right?" Jimmy asks.

"Yes . . . yes . . . it's upsetting. Pour me a little more brandy." Jimmy hurriedly pours the brandy (spilling some) and takes him the glass. "Don't ask me to explain why your mother left me . . . I can't tell you . . . I don't know . . . all Annette ever said was that she needed to feel secure. Maybe she had seen her parents killed . . . her mother and sisters raped . . . who knows? I don't know what terrible things may have happened to her as a child . . . and neither does she . . . she remembers nothing of her life in China. But she had decided to get rid of me, so she manufactured another father for her children, then killed him off and turned me into a distant relative."

"Why didn't you ever tell me?"

"How could I? What would I say? Besides, could you have understood? Even more to the point, would you have believed me?"

"Probably not," Jimmy admits. "But I wouldn't have been so confused when I was a kid." He is amazed to hear himself say this, even more amazed to discover that the intense dislike he has always felt for the man he must now recognize as his father has evaporated. Jimmy is enough of a realist, however, to concede that his change of heart is probably due to the almost instantaneous realization (assuming everything works out) that one day he stands to inherit a great deal of money and property. The prospect further weakens Jimmy's legs. "I have to sit," he whispers. He manages to reach a chair and crouch in it.

"Are you all right?" his father asks. "I could get my physician to look at you."

"No." Jimmy lies back, eyes closed. Behind his eyelids float glittering images of skyscrapers and obsequious bank employees. "I drink very little," he explains. " A beer now and then."

"I'm aware of your plebeian habits," his father dryly remarks. "Have you eaten today?"

"Not much," Jimmy says, making the most of his weak spell.

"I'll get my cook to fix you something. I'm surprised Annette let you out without nourishment."

"I wanted to get things cleared up." His dizziness subsides. Jimmy puts aside his dazzling future and sits up determined to deal with the present. "Do you know where Janet MacDougail is?" he asks.

His father goes to an intercom set in the wall, speaks into it and returns to sit across from Jimmy. "Before I tell you where I think she might be, I want you to explain why you broke into the MacDougails' home. And your reasons for following Peter MacDougail to Los Angeles and trespassing on his property."

"I was looking for Janet."

"Well, you thoroughly frightened Peter."

"He'll be even more frightened when he and his family are charged with drug trafficking."

"I'm afraid you have a lot to learn, James. Before you start making connections between the MacDougails and the drug trade, I want to tell you something about your own family's connection with it. Your great-great-great grandfather made a lot of money importing opium into Vancouver and your great-great grandfather a small fortune dealing in heroin and hashish."

"What about you?"

"Me? Oh, no . . . I'm a lazy, self-indulgent person . . . I risk nothing."

"Does that mean you're not involved in the drug trade?"

"It does. I happen to know Sergeant Robson gave you the FBI rundown on the MacDougail family. But before you pass judgment on them, just remember your ancestors supplied MacDougail companies with opium for their patent medicines. Oh, I know the FBI claims the MacDougails are still making millions from drug trafficking, and maybe there is a profitable little operation hidden away somewhere in their business empire, but if so, I'm not aware of it. And I doubt that Peter MacDougail is either—he's a man who's preoccupied with seeing and hearing no evil."

"So what about the cocaine in Martin MacDougail's apartment? Where did that come from?"

"I have no idea. I feel sorry for Margaret. Her sons were no good, and apparently the grandson was no improvement. Handsome men—maybe too good-looking—but weak. William, the older son, was an alcoholic before he even got out of school. And John didn't turn out much better."

"Were they drug dealers?"

"I doubt if they had wits enough for it. It's not surprising John managed to blow himself and his wife up on their boat. They spent a lot of time on it, drinking with their crowd. I went out with them once and swore I'd never do it again. John

MacDougail was the kind of man who'd throw a cigarette butt into a pool of gasoline, that's how reckless he was. For a while there was talk the explosion which killed him was deliberate, a way to keep him quiet, but nothing was ever proven."

"You mean nothing was proven about the explosion, or about their drug dealing?"

"Both. I'm of the opinion the brothers were being investigated simply because their name was MacDougail. Probably the Vancouver police were asked by the FBI to question them."

"Why didn't you explain this before?"

"Why should I? Better you find out for yourself. Poor Margaret. I think she suspected her grandson took drugs . . . but the family has no idea how Martin died or who killed the other two people. That's why Peter flew up to Vancouver, there were discussions with the police. Peter told me about his meeting with Robson. What could have possessed you to break into their house like a common thief? You must have been out of your mind!"

"I didn't break in. The side door was unlocked."

"You can indulge in fine distinctions if you like, but the police call it breaking and entering."

"Does Sergeant Robson know Peter MacDougail was in Vancouver?"

"Of course. Robson went to the Shaughnessy house to discuss the matter with Peter. Now I want you to listen to me, James. I must have told Annette a hundred times that she was doing you a disservice when she set you up in that miserable little office after your breakdown."

"It wasn't a breakdown," Jimmy protests. "I ran out of steam."

"Call it anything you please, I don't mind. But the fact is you've lost touch with reality. You've no idea what's going on in the world. How can you, when you spend all day gazing out your office window?"

This opinion angers Jimmy. He pushes himself out of the chair to say, "I know exactly what's going on. And I've built up a reasonably decent practice."

"Well, maybe you have," his father concedes. "You certainly aren't short of brains. But you have to get out of that dingy office. I've always given in to Annette and allowed her to have her way with you and your sisters, but things have to change. I'm going to insist you get experience in property development and financial management."

Jimmy ignores what his father says and asks again about Janet. "Tell me where she is."

"She's with her mother's family in West Vancouver.

"What's their name?"

"It's Murray, but I would advise you—"

"I don't want your advice on this matter." Jimmy says calmly. "I must talk to Janet. I have to find out what really happened. Don't you understand?"

"What I understand is you're in love with the girl and want to see her again."

"My feelings have nothing to do with it." Jimmy stops for a minute, then continues. "I think Janet killed her brother . . . and murdered two other people . . . and I have to find out why. I have to."

"My god! Are you certain of this?" Jimmy's father asks as a middle-aged man and woman enter the room, carrying large silver trays.

"Not absolutely," Jimmy replies. "But it's all that's left to conclude. That's why I must get an explanation from her."

Jimmy's father introduces Jimmy to the man and woman. "Mr. and Mrs. Chen, this is my son James." The couple nod and tell Jimmy they are pleased to make his acquaintance, although in fact Jimmy has already met them at Annette's store. The couple then place a table between the father and son and set the trays on it. "Thank you," Jimmy's father says as they bow slightly and leave the room. He uncovers bowls of soup. "Does Sergeant Robson also suspect Janet MacDougail?"

"He may. I'm not sure."

"Eat the soup, James. Indeed, I can see you're in a difficult position. Do you think Margaret MacDougail shares your suspicions?"

"I don't think so. But I could be wrong . . . I've made a lot of mistakes."

"Oh, I doubt if you've made many more than most inexperienced people do." Jimmy tastes the soup, discovers he is ravenously hungry. "Are you going to tell Sergeant Robson what you suspect?"

Jimmy stares down into the empty, beautifully crafted soup bowl. "I don't know what I'm going to do."

"Is there anything I can do to help? I could speak to Peter MacDougail."

"No. Please don't. And . . . Father . . . please don't speak of this to Mrs. MacDougail, or to Mother."

"As you wish. But please remember I am not without influence."

"Thank you," Jimmy says. "I should go." He stands, although his legs still feel wobbly. "Mother will wonder where I am."

"I'll walk with you, that is, if you don't object. I want to speak to Annette about a couple of matters."

They walk from the room to the elevator. Jimmy's father presses a button on the elevator panel. The door slides open and they enter the teakwood box to stand side by side.

"Did you send Evelyn Chan to me?" Jimmy asks.

"Let me see . . . I believe she asked me to recommend a lawyer to handle the settling of her husband's estate. I thought it would give you a little business. But I assure you I had no idea she would take you on as a lover."

The elevator descends, the door opens, they walk through the foyer and out into the street. "What are you going to do about Janet MacDougail?"

"I don't know. I'll talk to her first. Then I'll probably speak to Robson. I'll have no choice."

They walk for half a block before the older man speaks again. "I'm sorry . . . very sorry indeed." They walk on in silence until they cross a little park and enter Union Street. "You and I aren't exactly fortunate in our loves, are we?"

"Did you send Janet to see me?" Jimmy asks.

"No. That was a product of chance." His father takes
Jimmy's arm, detaining him. "Try not to worry too much,
James. It never helps." He smiles encouragement. "Now that
you know more about Annette and me perhaps we can do
something about changing our lives. I, for one, hope so."Together father and son proceed towards their encounter with
Annette.

12

Behind its mask of towering Douglas fir and coastal hemlocks the unpainted cedar-sided house seems small, and Jimmy thinks its original use might have been as a summer cottage. The Murray family could have come over from Vancouver by boat in the prosperous summers preceding the first great war. There is an air of genteel dilapidation about the place; rampant wisteria and clematis hang from trees, swarm over shrubs and cling to the sides of the house. Jimmy rattles the heavy, M-shaped, wrought-iron door knocker and waits until the door opens. A small, plump, middle-aged woman, whose national origin is practically certified on sight by a plaid skirt and hand-knit sweater, bids him good morning in a voice which still carries the lingering whisper of a burr. Jimmy proffers his business card and explains he has been told Janet MacDougail is visiting and might he please speak with her.

"Well, I don't know about that," the woman says.

"But she's here?" Jimmy prompts.

"Yes, but . . ."

"It's important. It's about her brother."

"Well . . ." She examines Jimmy's card and looks up at him, as if questioning his moral integrity.

"I have been investigating Martin's death for Janet. So I have legitimate reasons for seeing her."

"All right. She's at the front, down by the wharf. I'll take you around the side of the house."

The woman steps out of the doorway, closes the door, and leads Jimmy through the overgrown shrubbery, remarking that the protected southerly aspect of the grounds encourages profuse growth of all plant life on the property. They emerge onto a broad, grassy shelf from where they can look out across multitudes of breeze-generated wavelets to Point Grey, Lions Gate Bridge and the island-filled Strait of Georgia.

"You have a spectacular view," Jimmy remarks.

"Yes, it is. When the house was first built the family came by boat from Vancouver. The house is larger now. Everything else may have changed—but not the view."

Janet sits in an old wrought-iron chair, feet up on a low stone wall close to steps leading to a granite-block wharf. She hears the woman's voice and looks around. The sun has burnished her long hair and lent her skin the colour of dark honey. She smiles at Jimmy, whose heart pounds as he walks toward her.

"A visitor for you, Jan," the woman says.

When Janet stands, Jimmy sees she is wearing a two-piece swimsuit and that her hair is wet. "I finally got ducked, Auntie," she says, "but the water's freezing. Jimmy, this is my Aunt Mary, Mrs. Murray."

"We've been introduced," Mrs. Murray says. "Put something on, Jan dear. Remember how easily you burn." She nods in Jimmy's direction and enters the house through a set of French doors.

"How did you find me?" Janet asks, while Jimmy, acutely aware of the seductive curves of her body, politely turns away to look at the view, which now, after seeing Janet, he finds tedious.

"I asked around . . . and someone suggested you might be here." He cannot bring himself to look directly at Janet lest he reveal his desire and frighten her. The most he can bring himself to do is glance quickly at her, then turn away, but not before he sees how the sunlight reveals the down on her belly, and the strands of bronze-gold hair that curl from beneath the skimpy bikini bottom.

"I'll put something else on, Jimmy. If I don't, Aunt Mary will get after me. She's very old-fashioned. Doesn't think girls should wear bikinis. I won't be long." Although Jimmy thinks he ought not to, nevertheless he cannot prevent himself from watching the movements of her firm-fleshed buttocks. Before entering the house she turns to smile and repeats that she will not be long. Jimmy waits by the low wall, watching scoters and pigeon guillemots slide over the waves before suddenly disappearing beneath the water. He is not sure what he will say to Janet when she returns; a part of him regrets having to be here, but there is no alternative.

A door closes and Jimmy turns to watch Janet slowly walk from the house towards him. She carries a wide-brimmed sun hat and wears sandals and a bright, flower-patterned sun dress. "It's lovely here, isn't it, Jimmy?" she says, slipping her arm through his and moving so close he can feel the curve of her hip.

"Yes, yes it is."

"Aunt Mary doesn't have much money, so she may have to sell it. Of course, she'd get a lot for the house, but Aunt Mary says it'll break her heart if she has to leave. Maybe I'll ask Gran to buy it for me. We could live here."

She pirouettes and asks, "Do you like my new dress? Aunt Mary made it. She makes all her own clothes."

"She must be very clever."

"Oh, she is. It was a birthday present."

"When . . .?" Jimmy mumbles.

"Yesterday. Aunt Mary and I had a party."

"If I'd known it was your birthday, I would have brought you something."

"What?" She smiles, teasing him. "A bag of apples from your mother?"

"No. Something from me. Listen, Janet, I must ask you some questions."

She raises a hand and points to a promontory in the distance. "That's Lighthouse Park. Have you been there?"

"No."

"Once Martin and I swam out to it. I had to help him back, he got so tired. That was before I stopped loving him."

"Why did you kill him, Janet?"

She appears not to hear the question and suggests they walk down to the wharf. "Aunt Mary can't see us there," she says. She takes Jimmy's hand as they descend the broad steps to the wharf. "They can't afford a boat now. Isn't it a shame? Today was the first swim I've had this year. I had to force myself to dive in because I knew it would be freezing cold. Have you ever had to force yourself to do something, Jimmy?"

"Tell me about Martin."

"When did you find out?"

"I'm not sure. Perhaps I've known all along."

"I wish you didn't know."

"I often wished you'd never come to my office, Janet. Why did you?"

"I thought people would expect me to act in a certain way."

"You mean, they expected you to behave like a naive teenager out to prove her brother's death was an accident so that people wouldn't think badly of him for killing himself?"

"You believed me, didn't you?" She turns her head and smiles; her face is so close Jimmy can see all the gradations that make up the texture and colour of her skin.

"I suppose I did. Tell me what happened."

"Do you really want to know? Is it so important?"

"I have to know."

She sighs and slides her hand down his arm until it rests over his. "I thought Martin was the most wonderful person in the world."

She stops and Jimmy prompts her by murmuring a suggestive "Yes?"

"Why do people you trust let you go on thinking they're wonderful when they're really not?"

"I'm not sure. Perhaps they don't like to disappoint you."

"If that's true, then why do they do things they know will break your heart?"

"Is that what Martin did?"

"I don't see why I should say anything more." Her voice is flat and cold.

"You have to, Janet. I'm the one person in the world you can really trust. I love you, Janet."

She suddenly smiles, then rests her head on his shoulder. "And you won't ever hate me, will you? No matter what happens? No matter what I tell you?"

"I couldn't hate you."

She sighs, and when she speaks it is in a monotone. "When I was about twelve years old, Martin made me try on his clothes. I was as tall then as I am now, but I didn't have breasts and my bottom wasn't as big. We looked at ourselves in a mirror and we could have been twins, except for my long hair. Martin liked the way I looked in his clothes . . . he said they hid the ugly parts of my body. He told me to cut my hair or pin it up and he'd buy some wigs so I could disguise myself, and he would take me around with him at night. And so we did that. We'd go to parties and night-clubs, and he'd tell everyone I was his cousin from the States. It was fun . . . for a while. I'd go to his apartment on the weekends. Granny didn't know about it. She wouldn't have let me. She thought Martin was a bad influence on me."

"How did you get in and out without her knowing?"

"Through the side door. I have a key. It was easy."

"Did Martin do drugs?"

"I'm not sure. He . . ."

"What?"

"I didn't understand what was happening to him. He started acting funny . . . he seemed excited all the time . . . and he'd shout at people . . . and try to hurt them. It was scary. And he couldn't drive properly . . . he'd go through red lights and things like that. Once we hit somebody and I wanted him to stop, but he just drove on. He said it didn't matter . . . there were too many people in the world anyway. One night we ran into a tree near his apartment and smashed the car up. And another night when he was driving me home, he stopped the car and offered a lift to a girl . . . she wasn't very old . . . she was waiting at a bus stop. He told her he was going to drive me home first, then he'd take her where she wanted to go. When we got to our house, I left the car and started up the driveway . . . but Martin didn't drive away. I thought maybe something was wrong, so I went back." Her hand moves down to cover Jimmy's and convulsively squeeze it. "My brother was . . . wrestling with her . . . getting on top of her. It was awful."

She stops, and Jimmy removes his hand from hers and puts his arm around her shoulders as she leans against him, seeking comfort. "I didn't know Martin could do such a thing . . . Then he pushed her out of the car and drove off. She threw up on the sidewalk and then ran off. I felt bad . . . I still feel really bad . . . because I didn't offer to help her. I guess that's when I stopped loving him. I couldn't bear knowing Martin did things like that. Sometimes I thought . . . if he . . . if he did . . . things like that . . . with me . . . then maybe he'd leave other girls alone."

"Did Martin ever do anything to you?"

"I don't want to say . . . but he used to watch me when I was changing my clothes . . . and taking a bath . . . when I was younger. He'd come into my room and watch me getting dressed . . . and when I was getting ready for bed at night and he'd . . . sometimes he'd rub himself . . . he didn't, you know, take it out. But that stopped when I got older."

"He preferred young girls?"

"Yes . . . I didn't understand why. But he said he liked me a lot more when I wore boys' clothes."

"Did he like young boys?"

"I don't know. He'd say nasty things about my body . . . and about Betty Nelson's."

"You knew she lived with him?"

"Martin hated Betty Nelson. He told me he'd bet the man who lived with her that he could take her away from him. He said . . . Cow Tits . . . that's what he called her . . . would do anything for money. And she did move in with Martin, but he started to be mean to her right away . . . he wanted to get rid of her. He was always trying to hurt her feelings."

"He called you names too?"

"Yes . . . especially when he was . . . on edge."

"Why didn't you stop going out with him?"

"I wanted to . . . but I couldn't . . . I was afraid he'd do something real bad."

"Why didn't you tell your grandmother?"

"I promised Martin I wouldn't ever tell Gran about anything he did."

"But she knew he drank too much."

"Yes . . . but she didn't know about . . . the other things."

"Did she suspect he took drugs? Or that he sold them?"

"I don't know. Maybe she did."

"Did you know?" When Janet does not reply he asks her to tell him what happened the night Martin died.

"We went to the party."

"Betty Nelson was there?"

"Yes. She rushed over as soon as we got there and began screaming at him because he hadn't taken her out for dinner."

"What happened then?"

"Betty left, and we stayed for a while. Martin was drinking a lot. He said something to one of the women and she slapped his face. We left after that."

"Did you have anything to drink?"

"I pretended to . . . I always did that when I went out with Martin."

"What happened next?"

"We drove along Broadway . . . Martin saw some girls and he stopped the car. He got out . . . I didn't want to . . . he wouldn't listen when I asked him to please get back in the car. He went over to the girls . . . I don't know what they said, but after a few minutes he came back and asked me . . . if . . ." She stops and moistens her lips. "He asked me if . . . I . . . wanted to have sex with one of the girls . . . only he used different words . . . you know . . . I was really frightened . . . he'd never asked me to do that before. The girls laughed and Martin shouted at me, 'Come on! Be a man! Show 'em what you've got!' One of the girls yelled, 'Oh yeah, let's see what he's got.' Martin ran back and began hitting them. One girl fell down and he kicked her. That's when I got out of the car and ran over and pulled Martin back to the car. I wanted to calm him down . . . but I didn't know how to. I said we should go somewhere quiet and walk around for a bit. That's when Martin said we could go to Stanley Park and walk out onto the bridge. So that's what we did, and when we got onto the bridge, Martin climbed onto the—I don't know what it's called—"

"Balustrade."

"And I pushed him off. Afterwards I ran home."

"But Janet . . . why did you come to see me? The police had already determined Martin committed suicide. It was unnecessary to have me investigate his death."

"Betty Nelson telephoned me."

"This was before you came to see me?"

"She called twice. The first time she said she knew it was me at the party. When she called again I told her I'd hired you to find who Martin was with the night before he died."

"And what did she say?"

"She didn't believe me. She said if I didn't tell the police I was there, then she would."

"That was when you asked Betty to meet you at the house in East Vancouver?"

"I said we ought to talk things over."

"You and Betty both knew about the house?"

"Yes. Martin said it was his special place where he could do just as he pleased. He painted everything white . . . it was his favourite colour. He said white meant purity . . . like the bodies of boys and girls. He hung the picture of a naked girl on the wall . . . he said it reminded him of me when I was younger . . . before I became ugly. Betty told me Martin bragged to her about the things he'd done there . . . with girls . . . and with me. But that's not true. That was the way Martin talked when he was . . . not himself . . . or was drinking. It couldn't be true because Martin didn't like me any more . . . he told me I had changed into something ugly. And he said that our father had . . . done things . . . to him . . . and me . . . when we were little but that can't be true. I don't remember anything like that."

"Did you intend to kill Betty when you arranged to meet her at the house?"

"I thought she'd understand . . . but she wouldn't listen. She blamed me for her breaking up with Martin."

Janet shakes her head as if to throw off the memories in her mind. "I don't want to think about it any more. Let's talk about something else."

She points to a large white ship coming out of Vancouver harbour. "Oh, look! There's a cruise ship. Wouldn't it be great to sail on one of those? I read a story about a girl who went across the Pacific Ocean on a sailboat, all the way to New Zealand. New Zealand looked lovely in the drawings in the story. The girl said when you're in the middle of the ocean you forget everything that's ever happened to you in the past. That's what I'd like to do."

They stand together, watching in silence while the ship, filled with carefree people, passes. Images of himself with Janet, standing at the rail, looking down into blue-green tropical waters, Janet's long bronze-coloured hair floating in the breeze, flash through Jimmy's mind, but as the ship rounds a point of land and vanishes, he asks Janet if she took the heroin with her to the house in east Vancouver.

"No. Martin kept it there."

"The police search turned up nothing."

"I threw everything into a dumpster on Hastings Street before I got a taxi home."

"Did Martin keep sleeping pills there too?"

"Those were Gran's." Jimmy wonders if Janet understands how this statement condemns her, although even now he is not sure how much of what Janet has said is true and how much false. She is so practised a liar, so habituated to deceit, that a bald truth when uttered by her appears a lie, and an outright lie the sweet truth. While driving to the West Vancouver house, Jimmy had formulated several arguments which might be used to defend Janet in court, but he is of the opinion now that the only conceivable defence would be insanity, although he does not think Janet is insane according to any legal or medical definition he knows.

He asks himself whether there is any point in prolonging this painful interrogation, since it was going to happen again with Robson. But his need to know, the desire to have answers, drives him on. He listens in silence while Janet explains how she went to Martin's apartment to take away some clothes she kept there and to remove the bags of cocaine from beneath Martin's bed. She did not want the police to discover the cocaine because, she said, if they did, then nasty things about the family might be written in the newspapers. She regretted not knowing about the two bags hidden in the stereo speakers, since she could have taken them too and dropped them into the dumpster as she had done with the others.

"It's sad about the man who managed the apartment . . . but I was afraid he could identify me," Janet explains. When Jimmy makes no comment, she goes on to tell him that Martin had given her the gun and taught her how to use it because he wanted her to be protected in case of an attack by a mugger or rapist.

"Do you still have the gun?" Jimmy quietly asks.

"Oh no. I threw it away." She points to the water. "Far out there. I don't think anyone will ever be able to find it. The water's very deep." A breeze begins to blow inshore and Janet shivers.

"It may not matter," Jimmy says and tries to think of some way he can leave gracefully: he desperately needs to be somewhere by himself to sort through all the information he has received. Finally he tells her he must get back.

Janet does not try to detain him, but says she will walk him to the car. They go up the stairs together and cross the lawn to the French doors. She asks him to wait while she gets a jacket. Jimmy turns to watch a tug-pulled barge creep across the water. When Janet returns she is wearing her blue school blazer. She slips an arm through one of Jimmy's and they push through the shrubbery at the side of the house. "It's a bit like being in a jungle, isn't it?" she laughs. "Would you like to live in a place like this, far, far away from everyone, Jimmy?"

"Everyone except one person," he says. He looks into her face, the big grey-blue eyes, aware that the gun she claims to have thrown away nestles in the deep pocket of her blazer.

"Are you going to tell that awful Sergeant Robson what I've done? Will he put me in prison?"

"That's up to a court to decide, not the police."

They walk up the driveway and around the curve, where they are now hidden from the house. "You want to see my secret garden?" she asks, and when Jimmy nods, she pushes some rhododendron boughs aside and they pass into a shadowy plant world. Although Jimmy is aware that the road and the house are nearby, the enclosing mass of trees and shrubs prevents all sound from reaching them. "This is where Martin and I played as kids." She stops beside an old hollow cedar bole where a thick foam mattress has been placed between two of the tree's eroded buttresses. Janet laughs quietly. "We stole that from one of the spare bedrooms, and Auntie went around everywhere looking for it. It was really hilarious."

"I bet." says Jimmy, wondering if Janet has brought him here to kill him.

"You really love me, Jimmy?"

He can do nothing but stare at her, the answer written all over his face.

"We could . . . you know . . . no one would see us."

When Jimmy does not respond, she moves close and places her lips on his. He cannot stop himself from reaching under her dress to run his hands up the backs of her thighs. He tells himself that once he is released from his compelling need to join his body with hers there will be time enough to wonder why this is happening and to speculate at what moment Janet will take the gun out of her pocket and shoot him, for why else would she have brought it with her from the house? For the briefest of moments he wonders whether the consummation of his desire will match what he has imagined. Then all is forgotten as he kneels to lie with Janet on the mattress.

Afterwards Janet whispers in his ear, "You'll wait before telling the police, won't you?"

"Yes."

"Two or three days?"

"Three days."

"You promise?"

"Yes, I promise."

"I'd better go. Aunt Mary will wonder where I am. She fusses."

"Like Mother."

"Yes . . . like your mother."

They stand, and Jimmy turns away to hoist up and fasten his pants, then sneaks a look as Janet slips on her panties and pulls down her skirt.

"Give me the gun, please."

She takes the revolver from her pocket and hands it to him. "I would never have used it."

Jimmy wants to believe her but doesn't. They stand in the driveway looking at each other, and when she leans forward to touch his lips with hers, he whispers, "Don't . . . don't."

"I wish . . ." she begins, then swings away and races frantically around the bend toward the house.

Jimmy watches her go, then slowly walks to the car where, after putting the gun in the glove compartment and making sure the tape recorder in his pocket is turned off, he leans his forehead on the steering wheel and begins to sob.

♦　　♦　　♦

It is five years later, the present, and Jimmy stands at the window of the dingy room he once used as an office. He visits the place every year on the afternoon of the day he made love to Janet MacDougail in her shadowy, secret garden. He always positions himself at the window and, looking out onto East Pender Street, where people swarm like bees, he recalls the events of the MacDougail case, starting from the moment Janet MacDougail entered his office asking if she had come to the right place.

Although Jimmy is a level-headed sort of guy usually impervious to fanciful notions, he has come to believe that when he is physically present in his former office on this particular day of the year, a vision of Janet will materialize so pervasive and strong he will be able to see her standing in the doorway smiling at him. Although he realizes it is all just a little bit ridiculous, he is convinced that on this particular day, if on no other, he is somehow capable of communicating his great need for her.

Of course, being a reticent, careful man, he does not speak of his belief to other people. Yet that is not quite true: on one occasion, which he now regards as an example of misplaced confidence, Jimmy did try to explain to Sergeant Robson, whose ascent in the police hierarchy over a half-decade has been paralleled by the increase in the size of his gut, the reason he returns to the room every year. Robson, however, proved himself insensitive to Jimmy's psychic experiences, laughed derisively, and called it utter nonsense. Even now Robson cannot forget that Jimmy delayed three days before handing over the gun and the tape he had made of his final conversation with Janet. At the time, Robson bitterly castigated Jimmy, claiming his delayed adolescent sentimentality prevented the police from arresting a murderer. He does not accept Jimmy's explanation that Janet was an innocent victim, driven to commit murder by the emotional and sexual abuse of an older brother. Robson takes the opposite view; he asserts that Janet was a manipulative liar and a cold-blooded killer with an IQ (her school records prove this) matching Jimmy's, who encouraged her brother's pedophilic instincts, even his use of drugs, and when she saw he was on the verge of a breakdown, murdered him.

As the years pass, each man reinforces his own theory. Robson maintains Janet was the stronger of the two personalities and the instigator of whatever she and her brother did together; he claims Janet had to be centre stage, like all other psychos, which explains why she involved Jimmy in the first place—she was out to show him and the police just how smart she was. Jimmy counters by reminding Robson that Janet was terrified of her brother and of what he might do to her and to other girls; she had come to Jimmy because she felt guilty that she had been unable to prevent Martin from wrecking his life and the lives of other people and believed she had no choice but to kill him in order to stop his destructive behaviour; although she did not dare admit outright to having killed him, still she wanted Jimmy to uncover the truth because she hoped he would understand how she had felt and redeem her.

Whenever Robson and Jimmy get together they go over the same ground. First Robson has his say: "Listen, Mr. Sung, Janet MacDougail manipulated you from day one and you fell for it. That young woman is a killer and one of these days I'm going to catch up with her." Then Jimmy presents his case: "Listen, Robson, I don't question you know more about people who commit murder than I do, but you're wrong about Janet. It was not Martin who was on the point of breakdown, it was Janet. Martin had systematically stripped her of everything a child needs and values." Finally Robson offers a rebuttal: "Oh sure, Mr. Sung, but don't forget Martin MacDougail's not around to tell his side of the story." And on they go, each man firmly convinced his interpretation is the correct one.

Still, nowadays Robson treads carefully in Jimmy's presence, and there's no longer sarcasm in his voice when he calls him "Mister." Jimmy now effectively controls and will undoubtedly inherit almost two billion dollars worth of Vancouver real estate. Robson has let it be known among peers and subordinates in the police force that he is to be regarded as *the* authority on the Sung family, and whenever an opportunity arises he tactfully gathers as much information about them as he can: Is Lucille's husband's medical practice thriving? How is her new baby? Are Julie's twins getting on well at school? When are she and Bill expecting their baby? Is Annette keeping well? Does she miss not having a store to run? Is she still trying to get people to eat apples? And how is Mr. Sung, Senior? Enjoying living on Union Street? Still going to the race track with Sam Mackintosh?

But Robson is not openly inquisitive about Jimmy's private life; whatever he learns comes to him indirectly. He knows that during the past few years there has been a turnover of women in Jimmy's life, and that the female presently in residence at the enormous apartment—the one his father previously lived in, now occupied by Jimmy—is a young refugee from El Salvador. Robson is fascinated by the way Jimmy seems to be duplicating the sexual habits of his father; it reinforces his belief that people, whether they want to or not, are controlled by the reins of their genetic heritage. Now, whenever given an opportune moment, Robson likes to pontificate on the theme "like father, like son."

To Robson, Jimmy is a man who has everything and yet nothing, a man who exists in a cell of silence, a man for whom the most important event in the year is listening to a ghostly voice from the past accompanied by a twisted heart's beat of hope.

But for Jimmy this particular afternoon is different from the other anniversaries because of the pale blue airmail envelope which is resting in the inside pocket of his raw silk double-breasted suit. He has, just a few minutes earlier, found the envelope, with an Auckland, New Zealand postmark, in his box at the post office on Georgia Street. He has opened it while slowly climbing the twenty steps up to his office. There is no letter, just a colour photograph inside, a photograph of a beautiful young woman in her early twenties with full lips, high sculpted cheekbones, large grey-blue eyes and the most unusual long, bronze-coloured hair. On the back of the photograph are two words written with a felt-tipped pen: *Missing You.*